2035

PALMETTO
PUBLISHING
Charleston, SC
www.PalmettoPublishing.com

Copyright © 2024 by Aidan Hintze

All rights reserved

No portion of this book may be reproduced, stored in a retrieval system, or transmitted in any form by any means–electronic, mechanical, photocopy, recording, or other–except for brief quotations in printed reviews, without prior permission of the author.

Paperback ISBN: 979-8-8229-4933-1

2035

IN A WORLD ENSLAVED, FAITH IGNITES REBELLION

AIDAN HINTZE

CONTENTS

Prologue		vii
Chapter 1	David	1
Chapter 2	Mary	5
Chapter 3	Michael	8
Chapter 4	Samson	10
Chapter 5	Nathan	12
Chapter 6	Phillip	14
Chapter 7	Will	16
Chapter 8	Fallon	18
Chapter 9	The Dog	20
Chapter 10	To War	22
Chapter 11	The Shot Heard around the World	25
Chapter 12	Fallon	29
Chapter 13	David	31
Chapter 14	Mary	33
Chapter 15	Nathan	34
Chapter 16	Phillip	35
Chapter 17	Will	38
Chapter 18	Michael	41
Chapter 19	Phillip	43
Chapter 20	David	44
Chapter 21	Mary	46
Chapter 22	Nathan	48
Chapter 23	Brussels	50
Chapter 24	Michael	52
Chapter 25	Mary	54
Chapter 26	Ruiz	56
Chapter 27	Will	58

Chapter 28	Dietrich	60
Chapter 29	The Night Before	62
Chapter 30	Bolton	64
Chapter 31	Winters	67
Chapter 32	David	71
Chapter 33	Michael	74
Chapter 34	Bolton	76
Chapter 35	Winters	78
Chapter 36	Dietrich	80
Chapter 37	Ruiz	83
Chapter 38	David	85
Chapter 39	Michael	88
Chapter 40	Winters	90
Chapter 41	Dietrich	94
Chapter 42	Anderson	96
Chapter 43	Ruiz	98
Chapter 44	Mary	101
Chapter 45	Ruiz	107
Chapter 46	Michael	112
Chapter 47	David	118
Chapter 48	Bolton	126
Chapter 49	Dietrich	128
Chapter 50	Bolton	131
Chapter 51	Dietrich	134
Chapter 52	The Light at the End of the Tunnel	135
About the Author		137

PROLOGUE

In the year 2020, a cataclysmic event took place. It led to many years of death, destruction, and global changes in power centers. Eventually, a small conclave of individuals was able to create a global government, with everyone from every nation under its umbrella. The world started to shift, and life became more "normal." This one-world government ushered in a new way of thinking, a new way of governing. People need not be concerned with political dogfighting anymore, as we now have one governing force that always does the right thing. The world has never been better for all who comply.

This story will follow the lives of different people living in various parts of the world in the year 2035. Some came from poor families, some from middle-class backgrounds, and some from wealthy ones. But none of that matters now, as there exists only one class.

CHAPTER 1

DAVID

The sun was shining brightly, so brightly that David was unable to sleep in on his day off. As he awoke, he went downstairs to the kitchen, following his normal morning routine of making coffee and having a light breakfast. To his dismay, for the first time all week, Katie and Jack had beaten him to the kitchen. They had purposes that allowed them to work from their shared apartment, so they seldom woke up as early as he did. Regardless, he would just wait for them to finish using the kitchen supplies, hoping they would be done before their preplanned morning rental ran out.

This new way of living was amazing, way better than before, but David sometimes felt rushed to use the kitchen supplies since they were all rented. He understood why the experts (the "experts" are people with expertise in a given field, the government vets them extensively to make sure they don't have any religious or "terrorist" sympathies, and if they don't, and are willing to forward the agenda of the New World Government, they are given high status and a good life) said it was better this way, and it was free! He just wished the time limits weren't so short.

When Katie and Jack were done, it was David's turn to make his breakfast. He opened the fridge and asked, "Jack, where is the avocado?"

"Sorry, man, had the last one."

David thought, "Well, I guess that's no big deal. Our groceries will reset in three days anyway."

After breakfast, David thought of going for a walk outside in the park. As he was leaving the shared three-bedroom apartment (with bunk beds in each room to sleep six), he saw the marketing team from Omarion

Corp walking in. They were a little late today, but they took over the living room from 8:00 a.m. to noon for their business operations. No private ownership was one of the genius ideas the experts gave them. It was a big part of why they all lived for free. They owned nothing, so everything was given to them by the Government. The only downside was the experts chose who got to enter the apartment during daylight hours. Business meetings were allowed all throughout the day, but David particularly liked the Omarion crew, mostly because Lucy worked for them.

The experts gave them housing because it was their right, along with food and a purpose (a job, which they called a purpose because it was determined by the experts based on a test you would take). It was a relief for everyone not to worry about bills anymore like they used to. Everyone was debt-free. They didn't have to worry about transportation because they were given housing close to their purposes. (Everything was within a fifteen-minute walk in these newly designed cities. It was genius!) They didn't have to worry about food because their plant-based diets were automatically dropped off to them weekly. David thanked science for that. Before this, people thought eating meat was okay! However, the experts showed them that meat was very bad for them, so they determined their food and caloric intake based on what best suited their purposes. This made life very simple and allowed them to focus on their purpose and leisure.

David couldn't wait to get to the park. He got lucky this week as his day off from work lined up with his park pass. Every citizen received a weekly park pass, allowing them access. To limit the spread of viruses and diseases, the experts didn't want too many people there at once, which was smart. David appreciated that it meant he wouldn't be bothered at the park. It was perfect! Some people thought they should be allowed to talk to more than one person at a time, but they clearly weren't in an area affected by the pandemic like David was. He would do anything the experts said to avoid that happening again.

While at the park, David saw a dog. Dogs were not allowed in society anymore, as they could spread diseases. Further, they could snap at any moment and kill people. David immediately called the police about the dog. While the police were on their way, David saw a young teenager chasing after the dog, yelling a name.

David warned the boy to go away or the animal would kill him, but the boy kept chasing the dog. He eventually caught the dog, and David knew it was this boy who had put them all at risk. He scolded the boy and promptly pointed him out to the police to ensure the safety of society. The police thankfully took the boy and the dog away. Hopefully, the boy learned his lesson.

Because of the Disease Spreading Animal Act of 2032, no one was allowed to own any animal. The experts released thousands of documents detailing cases of humans becoming sick from their pets and spreading illnesses. What was left out of these reports was that the vast majority of these illnesses came from desperate families who were forced to eat their pets. As with all totalitarian regimes, the truth was laden with lies.

David went back to his shared apartment as his park pass reached its limit. When he got back inside the apartment, he saw Katie and Jack sitting in the living room. The Omarion group had concluded their meeting and left, so they had roughly one hour before the next group would use the living room as a conference room. David sat with Jack and Katie, and they tuned on the television.

The televisions had one hundred channels, each thoroughly reviewed by the experts to ensure there was no conspiratorial information. They decided to watch a program about how fortunate the world is. Like many such programs, this one opened with a moment of silence for the 6.5 billion lives lost, then a moment of appreciation for being among the 1 billion left on Earth, and further appreciation if you were 1 of the 30 million people who still had the ability to reproduce.

They said the pandemic had ended, but it seemed viruses were stronger now than ever. People would sneeze one day and be gone the next! No one really knew what was going on. Maybe we were evolving backward. That was why David, like most do, really appreciated the experts who continued to do everything to keep them safe and living. The experts told them soon they would be out of this. The beauty of it all was they had already created a perfect world for people to live in, with the right amount of structure and free—err, purpose. The *F* word was forbidden now, as too many crazies used it and took it too literally. But the experts had created the perfect world for everyone to live in, for when the viruses weakened or the bodies became stronger.

CHAPTER 2

MARY

Mary had bought her apartment in 2022, in the midst of the pandemic. She worked hard to pay off her mortgage, achieving this by 2026, even with the world split nation by nation in civil conflict. Then in 2028 the talk about eliminating all private ownership began, and by 2030, with all the "purposes" being placed in populated areas, every apartment within a one-hundred-mile radius was confiscated by the government. Mary's two-bedroom, two-bathroom apartment, which she had worked for, was now split among four people—herself, Janice, Samuel, and Brad.

Apartments outside the one-hundred-mile radius of a major population center were also confiscated by the experts. But they were all converted either into sustainable energy sources, such as wind farms and solar farms, or into regular farms to grow vegetables. There are theories that some of the land outside the one-hundred-mile radius also had camps for noncompliant people, but that was just a rumor. The experts assured that everyone complied because it was a system that truly benefited everyone.

While Mary was initially upset about having to share the apartment she had worked for, she grew to understand this was for the greater good. After a few months, she no longer complained, especially after the experts gave her a clerical purpose at the new central government building in the heart of Lexington. The experts told everyone all purposes were equally important, but the only purpose where one could actually see a rise in their quality of life was if they worked in the central government buildings. One could make a name for themselves there and get to a higher purpose and might even be rewarded with a house.

AIDAN HINTZE

The houses were very few and far between, but they were the only way for living alone or with just one's family these days. Everyone understood the waste was too much, and the planet was dying. The experts had showed everyone the faults in their ways, but Mary missed being able to wake up and not be immediately in the presence of others. Also, she hoped to be a mother one day, and with the apartment already crowded with four people, adding a child and, God willing, if the experts' wisdom showed Mary the way, a husband would make the apartment feel even smaller.

Mary was on the list for the experts to set her up with her "perfect match." The experts had an amazing success rate—100 percent of couples they matched together stayed together! Divorce had been eradicated because of the experts' wisdom. But the process took a long time and required a payment of sixty labor credits (equivalent to sixty hours of overtime work)—a price Mary was more than willing to pay to find a suitable husband and have children. She had been so happy three months ago when she found out that she was among the thirty million who were still fertile. However, many had told her she still should not have children, arguing that even with the current number, the world was still too populated. But being a mother had been Mary's dream all her life, and somehow she was fortunate enough to still have that ability after everything, so she decided she was not going to throw that away.

After a six-month searching process, the experts would allow the pair they had made to meet at a location of the experts' choosing. The beauty of this arrangement was the meal would be free. Grocery stores were already free, but some top-tier restaurants would require credit hours, which were only earned if one worked beyond their shift. But the experts were nice enough to pay so the couples could meet.

After the first meeting, if both parties wished to have another, they were allowed an extra thirty-minute park pass to speak further to get to know each other. After that they would have to decide whether they wished to be wed. The third date only happened if they both agreed to be wed. After they both agreed, the third meeting was a trip to the cinema.

Most cinemas were gone now, but they kept a few in operation specifically for this purpose. The couple got the entire cinema to themselves.

The experts would then set up a wedding, where they would allow five family members from each side to attend. This wasn't a big deal, as most families were small now anyway. Mary couldn't wait for the day they find her match. She had been waiting for three months and writing in her journal about how she imagined him to look nightly. They were not supposed to have journals or write about the future or hopes. The experts said hope could be dangerous and manipulated. It was what caused the world uprising of 2027! Mary thanked the experts that the good people of the world were able to win and give everyone this amazing world.

Marriage was outlawed for multiple reasons, chief among them being when people truly marry out of love, they might act out of emotion for each other rather than logic. They would be willing to choose them over the state or the needs of society. Further, that love became compounded when they had children. It was much easier to force adoption on a couple chosen by the government than on a couple who met on their own and had a real connection. The New World Order (NWO) knew there would always be the risk of the couples they set up growing real attachments, which was why they gave them homes outside the city; they could be more easily monitored there and taken out without anyone knowing if necessary.

CHAPTER 3

MICHAEL

Michael was a noncompliant one. The areas one hundred miles outside the major population centers were his hiding grounds, and he was far from alone. While most of the world chose to comply for a multitude of reasons, some thought it would be a better world and truly believed in what they were being told. Others believed resistance was futile and hopeless. Some felt nothing would actually change. Most assumed someone else would do it for them.

Michael was a part of the Charlamagne Division, which consisted of thousands of noncompliant ones who lived their lives without the rules and regulations the experts put on the rest of the world. Michael and the Charlamagne Division had to camouflage where they lived to avoid being spotted by drones or by satellite imagery. They often lived underground in caves or on mountain ranges, where they could use stealth technology they had developed. This technology in essence mirrored the imagery behind them and projected it in front of them, allowing them to go undetected by drones.

The Charlamagne Division was one of thousands of resistance movements spread out across the globe. It was the most notorious because when the world uprising happened, many of its members, including its founder, were sent in to quell the rebellion inside the city of Lexington. However, the leader and his men joined the people and helped them set up a defense that thwarted the experts' military forces for close to three years. The conflict only ended when the experts began killing civilians in the city through fire bombings of population centers and homes.

The Charlamagne Division could not live with the innocence dying en masse, so they offered anyone who wished to come with them, urging them to follow. They broke a hole through the forces surrounding the city and were able to escape. At the beginning the Charlamagne Division fielded close to sixty thousand men. By the end their military numbers had dwindled down to ten thousand, but they had gained approximately one-third of the city's population following and joining them, boosting their numbers to a formidable eighty thousand.

Michael was one of the civilians who opted to go with the Charlamagne Division. His mother did too. His father and sister were killed in the bombings by the experts, but his brother, Elijah, chose to stay. He said he wanted to forget it all and live a normal life, not a life on the run. Michael felt this "life on the run" was the only way to live now, and after two years of living this way, he realized something incredible.

The entire Charlamagne Division was very close-knit, as they had to be, relying on one another for survival. They also learned and taught holistic and centuries-old approaches to life, health, and education, among other aspects. Michael felt like he was not on the run, but rather, he was actually living exactly as we are all supposed to, not locked in the rat race of the "modern world" as he was before the great uprising. He was also not a slave to this new world, but rather, he was free. He had never felt closer to his ancestors, to humanity, and most importantly, to God.

The Charlamagne Division, like all resistance groups, was known as a "terrorist organization" to the experts and those who lived inside the city centers. The division struggled with the idea of just attempting to hide out and build their own little world, leaving those who walked themselves into slavery to fend for themselves or to fight to bring a free world to them, even though they would not fight for it themselves.

Despite the many inner debates in the division, it was run as a democracy, and thus, a majority voted to wage a conflict against the experts and attempt to free those living in the city centers from the tyranny imposed upon them. However, it was a small majority; of the 80,000 total members, the final vote was 42,761–37,239.

CHAPTER 4

SAMSON

Samson, a broad-shouldered Goliath of a man who stood 6'4" and weighed 260 lbs., was the top general in the Charlamagne Division. His body looked as if it were sculpted by Michelangelo, with every muscle defined to perfection. He was a gentle giant, at least to those on the division's side. He stated very plainly that no one would be forced to participate in any action in this conflict. It would be an offensive force consisting of volunteers only.

This decision was made not only because he believed it was the right thing to do but also because he understood they could not take on the experts' military with the numbers and the equipment they had. So they would have to fight this war as the American War for Independence and so many others were fought, with small guerrilla movements, striking supply lines, drawing them out into ambush grounds, and so on.

To be successful in a grueling campaign like this, one's heart needed to be fully in it. Most of the men in the division were faithful of all faiths and denominations—Christians, Jews, Muslims, Buddhists, and other religions. Samson understood that faith in God was important, but he needed warriors who had faith in their cause as well.

Samson had lived a good life before the war. He graduated from West Point the top of his class and had his stars within two years after graduation. He came from a long line of soldiers with a proud lineage. Samson had two brothers, Jackson and Killian, and two sisters, Kiera and Erin. Jackson and Killian also followed their family's lineage and joined the military once they were of age. Kiera and Erin sought different paths until the war started, and then they answered the call. They would say it was because of their big brother or their close family loyalty to one another, but most in the division believed it was just in their blood to fight, and they couldn't deny their ancestors any longer.

That was a major difference between the outer settlements and those in the cities. The outer settlements believed in honoring one's lineage, ancestors, and God or gods—it didn't matter if one believed in multiple. They did not put their faith in humans but rather in a higher power that called them to walk their paths. That was what gave them all faith in their ultimate victory. The NOW soldiers they would be marching against may have had better weapons, more money, more soldiers, but they lacked a faith in something more powerful than themselves, and that made them weak and vulnerable.

CHAPTER 5

NATHAN

Nathan was always a well-liked man. As a child of a large family from Lexington, he had three brothers and four sisters. Nathan's family was torn at the onset of the pandemic, with some choosing to listen to the experts, take the vaccines offered, and follow their advice, while others chose their own path. Nathan was unsure which path to truly take; he just wanted the infighting within his family to end.

Until his sister Bianca became ill. She had been pushing the entire family to get the vaccine, and she was the first in line. Bianca died of a sudden heart arrhythmia just two days after receiving her vaccine. The family was assured this was due to something other than the vaccine. Nathan's mother and father both got the vaccine, as did one of his three brothers. Within two months, all of them were dead.

Even though Nathan was constantly assured the vaccine could not have caused this, he sought his own information and answers. He had never been outspoken about anything until this, and it would eventually cost him.

After the great uprising, questioning any official source was outlawed under punishment of exile. Or so everyone was told. Nathan believed the biggest risk he was running by speaking out was he would be banished to live on the outskirts among the rebels, an idea that he did not want but also did not mind. The reality was much worse.

Nathan's two brothers and three sisters were "exiled" first, which made Nathan now completely willing to be exiled, considering they had never spoken out. Then the white hats came for Nathan. To Nathan's dismay they did not drive him to the outskirts to join the Charlamagne

Division, or the Tenth Legion, or any of the "rebel" groups. Instead, he was driven to a desolated area in the midst of a forest where he saw a massive camp.

On the front gate of the campsite, the words "your purpose is your work" were written in Latin. Nathan saw more people than he had ever seen before, all cramped together, clearly malnourished. Now fear began to set in. He hadn't realized this was the consequence for his actions. He prayed quietly, of course, so the white hats wouldn't hear, hoping that since he was the only one who had spoken out, his family would at least be spared this fate.

Then his worst fear was realized when he saw his remaining brothers and sisters in the camp. All of them had clearly lost weight and were barely recognizable. One of his sisters had just gotten married and had a child. Since the NWO didn't allow divorce, her husband and newborn daughter were in the camp with them, all because of Nathan's disobedience.

CHAPTER 6

PHILLIP

Phillip had always been a career man in the military, ready and willing to do whatever he had to for a promotion. He had a terrible reputation among his subordinates but a stellar one among his superiors, as was often the case with poor leaders.

Phillip joined the military in 2017 at the age of eighteen, saw some action at the end of the Afghanistan war, and was investigated for an incident where over one hundred civilians were murdered on suspicion of a potential ambush. While being investigated, the military put him in charge of a prison for suspected terrorists. Because of an internal military investigation, it was found during his time overseeing this prison that inmates were forced to perform sex acts on each other. (Many were devout in their religious faiths.) Those who refused would be attacked by the working dogs at the facility, targeting those inmates' genitals.

Phillip was charged with wrongdoing but was never convicted. It was speculated this was because he had made unsavory friends in high places. Still, the US Army gave him a less-than-honorable discharge. When the civil war broke out, Phillip was given an opportunity to join the military again. The NWO leadership decided they needed a man with his talents. His reputation only grew, and for good reason.

Phillip grew up in a small town in the northeast named Bennington, just outside Massachusetts. When the war initially broke out, Massachusetts was undecided about which side to join. The NWO gave Phillip command of an elite force made up mostly of European commandos with one purpose: to put fear in the hearts of anyone who would dare stand against the NWO.

It turned out Phillip was the perfect man for the job. Within a week of his assignment, his unit had burned to the ground every small town in Massachusetts that had ever voted for anti-establishment politicians. Phillip started with his own hometown. Many people he grew up with and went to school with still lived there, but that did not matter to Phillip. He had his orders, and he was going to fulfill them.

While this was seen as an astounding success by the NWO, with the votes going 92 percent in favor of joining the NWO, it also had another effect. Massachusetts had a remaining population of one million people before Phillip's campaign. Phillip brutality massacred roughly one hundred thousand of them and caused another two hundred thousand to flee and join rebel groups.

While the NWO figured this wouldn't matter, as they had one of the most populated remaining states in the fold now, they had also seen the measure of this man's brutality. However, this would come back to haunt them.

Phillip's brutality got him a massive promotion. He was named as the officer in charge of the new work camp that was being built outside Lexington. This new position came with a new rank, a new uniform, and a much bigger responsibility. Now Phillip was in charge not only of military personnel but also of civilian (slaves) who were required to make certain work quotas. While Phillip's job description changed, his tactics certainly did not.

CHAPTER 7

WILL

Will was a police officer in Boston when everything went to hell. It started with the pandemic, which Will worked through, often working twelve-hour shifts, seven days a week. One year after the onset of the pandemic, Will was told he would be forced to get the vaccine or be fired. Will had never been antivaccine, but he didn't understand; he was fine working through the pandemic with no personal protective equipment and never caught the disease once.

Will had been on the most COVID-19-sensitive tasks. They had designated COVID-19 jails where they would send cops willing to go to, and Will was always sent. He was constantly in contact with people who had COVID-19 and had never caught the disease or taken a single sick day because of it. So this decision did not sit well with Will.

After months of debating the pros and cons, Will decided to leave the force rather than take the vaccine, a choice that very well might have saved his life. Shortly after Will made this decision, it was announced that anyone not vaccinated would be sent to certain "zones" where they could live among other unvaccinated individuals.

Will was a student of history, and he saw an eerie similarity between this and what the Nazis had told the Jewish people. He decided to convince as many family members as he could to head for the hills in the hopes they could start a new life and live off the land. Will was married to a Swedish woman named Lagothar, has a son named Steven, and has two brothers named Mitchell and Henry. All but Henry decided they would go with Will.

When the war broke out, Henry showed up to the homestead that Will and the rest of them had built. Henry told him of the horrors happening in the city and of what Phillip, a man Will had grown up with and called a friend, did to their hometown just outside Boston. Despite Lagothar's pleas, Will decided he couldn't sit idly by. He knew waging open war against the military with a handful of people was suicide, so his plan was simple: offer anyone who wished to join a place on his homestead.

He never imagined in his wildest dreams the number of people would take him up on his offer. Thus, the largest of the rebel groups was born: the Massachusetts Minutemen.

CHAPTER 8

FALLON

Fallon grew up poor on the outskirts of Lexington. When the NWO takeover began, his family rejoiced, and they were skyrocketed to a much better life. Sure, they had to share their living space and cooking supplies, but this was better than being a paycheck away from being homeless.

Fallon's parents taught him well. Unlike most who grew up poor and benefited from the NWO system, he did not have any disdain for those who were upset about being brought down a class or even by those who chose to flee and live on their own. He was taught everyone had their reasons for doing what they did and not to hate or judge them for it.

Fallon took this to heart. It was evident throughout his time in the NWO military. While everyone was forced to do something for the NWO, the military was Fallon's idea of giving back to the group that had given his family so much. He was very much beloved by his subordinates. Where many others in this structure had a "shit rolls downhill" mentality, Fallon had a "the shit stops at my rank" mentality. He would take the arrows for his men, and that did not go unnoticed.

Fallon also had a reputation among the rebels that was very favorable. While he was respected as a strong warrior and leader, no one would ever accuse him of being harsh or cruel. Even when ordered to annihilate cities, he would refuse, a risk that would normally have an NWO leader killed. However, the superiors feared doing so would cause many lower-level troops to defect, and rightfully so.

Fallon was stationed inside the city of Lexington and was very well-known by the residents. He would talk to anyone who looked like they needed a friendly face or an ear to listen to them.

CHAPTER 9

THE DOG

David received an email from the police chief, thanking him for the countless lives he saved by reporting that disease-spreading animal. He also received an extra hour at the park from the experts as a reward and was granted leave to have his own room for the night at a hotel of his choosing.

David was very excited, but he told everyone he would have done it even without the rewards, as it was just the right thing to do. He couldn't wait to use his extra hour at the park, so the next morning when he woke up, he skipped breakfast and went straight there.

When he got to the park, he saw a woman crying. He knew the rules well; he could speak to someone if it was just a one-on-one conversation, if they stayed eight feet apart. (Six feet was too close; the experts realized later it needed to be eight. If only they had realized sooner, so many lives would have been saved!)

He safely approached the woman and asked if he could help her. The woman did not respond; she just kept crying and staring at something in her hand. David asked again if he could help comfort her, but he got no response.

He inched closer, trying carefully not to break the eight-foot barrier but desperately attempting to see what was in her hands. He finally got close enough. It was a picture of a little boy. David was confused. He asked her if the boy in the picture was missing, to which the woman finally responded.

The woman told him that her son had a severe anxiety disorder and was very socially awkward, but he always felt comfortable and open around their family dog. She knew it was against the antidisease laws enacted in 2028, but she had to keep the dog for her son so he would have a chance at a normal life. But the dog escaped, and the son knew the punishment for the dog would be death, so he chased after it.

The police told her they found her son with the dog in the park, thanks to a Good Samaritan. But the punishment for possessing the dog was the same as the dog's punishment, so they sent her back his ashes. She said they didn't even give her the chance to bury her son.

David was unsure how to feel. He definitely did not feel sorrow, remorse, or even empathy. Empathy, the emotion that most of the goodness of humanity was based on, was being systematically eradicated by the experts. This was by design.

Sure, it was sad her son died, but David had no choice; he was doing his civic duty. Her son should have been taught better than to have a disease-spreading animal. He thought, "So what if you have anxiety? What about my health?"

If anything, David now felt anger toward the woman for ruining his time at the park with her nonsense. This was why the experts said it was best to give children up for adoption and take on someone else's so these silly attachments didn't cloud judgment. Society's needs must come before any individual person or family. David thought, "This is what the experts say, and it is how I live my life."

CHAPTER 10

TO WAR

Michael and his unit were gathering all their gear when they heard the drums, which hadn't been used in a war in a long time. As stated previously, these warriors believed in the power of the olden ways. The drums were used to keep step in march, to amplify their size at times to enemy scouts listening, but mostly to pay homage to their ancestors and summon them to join the fight beside the living.

These drums were used to summon all the legions of the Charlamagne Division. They all went to the field where Samson was waiting, perched up slightly on a makeshift wooden platform structure.

Samson waited for all his men to file into the field before he began.

"Men, women, warriors, today, we embark on a journey many before us have made time and again. As the Jews did in the ancient lands against the Egyptians. As the Spartans did against the Persians. As the Britons did against the Romans. As our forefathers on this American land did against the British as well. We have been called terrorists, and likely we will be called worse in the days, months, years to come. I will not tell anyone to die where they stand, but know that surrendering will likely mean torture, and I would rather not die the way the Cossack warriors did. They will call us many things and treat us horridly if captured. But I need each and every one of you to look to your families, look to your hearts, and above all, look to your God or gods.

"We know why we fight this war. This is a fight of liberation. This is a fight that no matter what the history books will in time say, we know why we're marching. We know what's waiting for us, and we march anyway for our families' sake, for humanity's future's sake, for God's sake. I will not ask anything of you I am not willing to do myself, which is why as your commander, I will be in the vanguard of our assault.

"We will be marching in one hour. Say your goodbyes to your families as I will mine because most of us will not return. Keep their memories close. We will need it for the fight to come. But when the fight starts, I want you thinking of two things, and two things alone: saving the warrior beside you and killing the bastard in front of you. *No quarter asked and none given!*"

Michael and the men were as excited as they'd ever been. They'd all seen combat before, so they knew the horrors of it. That was not why they were excited. They were excited because this was the first time in the war that they were taking the fight to the enemy, going on the offensive. While it hadn't been confirmed, there were rumors they were not the only one. It could just be a morale-boosting rumor, but the tale went that Samson waited this long for an offensive because he was building lines of communications with the other divisions and were planning to attack every metro center in the United States simultaneously. If it was just a morale-boosting rumor, it worked. The men went from thinking it a suicide mission to telling their families that they would be home in three months and that they would be living in a free America again.

Hundreds of miles to the east of the Charlamagne Division, word had reached the Massachusetts Minutemen: the march had begun. While they had a great appreciation for their ancestors, the minutemen did not have drums, nor were they seen as faithful in God as the Charlamagne Division or many other rebel groups. The minutemen were driven simply by a duty to their fellow man and their desire to be left alone by an overreaching, overbearing government.

The minutemen were by far the largest rebel group, boasting a total force size of 160,000, large enough to take on the NWO force based inside Boston. However, the rebel force was made up of people of all walks of life, and not all of them had much experience in combat or a background in firearms. Nevertheless, the time was upon them to march to war, and everyone did.

Word had now reached Samson that seventeen of the nineteen major rebel groups were on the move toward their targets. He had not received any word back from the other two, but it did not matter; this mission did not need to win a single one of the seventeen battles on the verge of taking place for it to be successful, and Samson knew this. Most of the people inside these cities did not believe others were still existing. They did not believe there was another option.

This was why every rebel group had similar orders. Throughout the fighting the first and main targets were the access points to the major metro areas. As of now no one could leave a metro area; the access points were flooded with concertina wire, machine gun nests, and land mines. While the main force of each rebel group began a skirmish with the NWO forces, their special operators would be making exfil points throughout the cities and freeing as many people as possible. That was the true purpose of this mission.

CHAPTER II

THE SHOT HEARD AROUND THE WORLD

The first shots of the conflict rang out in Dallas, Texas, where the Alamo Division, while severely outnumbered, was dealing a massive blow to the NWO. Word reached Samson that the Alamo Division was actually having major success in this battle. Samson almost hesitated to believe the information, thinking it must be some NWO trick.

The Alamo Division, mostly made up of seasoned soldiers, only had five thousand men, yet they were taking on an NWO force of thirty-five thousand entrenched in solid fighting positions. Samson read the news to his lieutenants and had them disperse it among the men. Whether he believed it or not, the men needed it, and their battle was only minutes away.

As promised, Samson was on the front line. The tanks of the Charlamagne Division were really just tractors with RPGs affixed to them, but they did the trick. Seven Charlamagne "tanks" blasted a hole in the front gate to the city of Lexington. The NWO personnel were caught by surprise, which was confounding to Samson. He knew they had drone flights and radar systems. How could they be caught off guard? He didn't care to think of it. His men knew their orders, and the fight began.

Samson was leading a squad of soldiers through the breach made in the front gate. As they pressed through, they encountered a few squads of NWO personnel, but it was not what they were expecting. There was tougher fighting on the east and south walls, which was also where the special operators were sent because those were the major access points.

Samson and his men made it within two miles of the city center and took up positions in buildings surrounding it. At this point they had already liberated much of the city, but Samson knew the NWO's largest force in the States was encamped here.

Samson tried not to, but he felt overjoyed. He couldn't believe they had achieved such an astounding victory and were on the verge of actually capturing the city center.

Michael was now scrambling to reach Samson. The building they were all in was just struck by a myriad of fire from Apache helicopters. Samson was directly in front of the window one of the Apaches was firing into. Michael sprinted to Samson's body and attempted to drag it away until he was pulled off by other members. They all loved Samson, but he was dead, and they had a fight to win.

With only two years of experience and training in any form of combat, Michael was not only considered elite in the division but was also one of Samson's most trusted men. Because of this, when the division decided their top general needed men with him to protect him at all times, Samson insisted that Michael be among them.

Michael had proven himself to be a solid warrior in the past two years. But no one expected to see this side of him. He was enraged at seeing this leader, whom they all loved, killed, and he was seeking vengeance. Samson's last order was to hold in the surrounding buildings in an attempt to negotiate a ceasefire with the remaining NWO militants. Michael no longer liked this idea.

As Samson's trusted man, when Michael gave the order for a charge forward, no one questioned it. Most knew that since Michael had just given an order, Samson had perished, and they were happy to die alongside him.

Samson's order to hold wasn't just to spare NWO lives; it was Samson who had previously ordered to give no quarter. Samson's order to hold was because he knew there had to be a reason why the NWO soldiers gave up the outer defenses so easily. Now the entire division would learn that reason.

The Charlamagne Division was battle-hardened. They had fought and seen the horrors of war before, but nothing prepared them for this. Almost as if with the flip of a switch, as the Charlamagne Division charged toward the city center, the street seemed to flip upside down. When it did, crucified bodies were now atop the street, with people still living and crying out for help. Hundreds, thousands, tens of thousands. All were women and children.

Most in the Charlamagne Division stopped their charge at the sight of this. Many started attempting to untie the people crucified, but the crucifixions were laden with proximity explosives. Some decided to hunker back down in their buildings. But Michael and the rest of Samson's unit seemed unfazed; they were focused on the tower in the center of the city.

If their intel was correct, that tower housed all the command and control for the NWO and Lexington. It was Samson's prized target. If the battle could be won, that tower could be used to communicate instantly with the other rebel divisions. It could also be used to take control of the drone squadrons and use the automatic shutoff for the manned aircraft now doing sorties over their positions.

Michael and his men miraculously made it to the tower, where they now had to face the most well-trained NWO troops in close-quarters combat. Luckily for Michael, Samson's unit was all ex-special forces and had extensive training and experience in this.

The NWO army was formidable in open spaces and anywhere their air superiority, superior weaponry, equipment, and technological advances could give them an advantage. But when it came to close-quarters combat, the rebel forces had the edge.

Michael's unit systematically made their way through the tower, clearing room by room, leaving a wake of bodies in their path. They executed constant Zimbabwe drills, a technique they had trained often, which involved shooting a target twice in the chest and once in the head. Since it was a small unit, and they couldn't afford to be engaged from behind, they'd often give the enemy combatant a few extra in the head as they stepped over them for good measure.

Upon seeing muzzle flashes going off inside the tower, all the remaining Charlamagne Division men on the outside began to push to the city center, where the main NWO force was still entrenched. Their advance was slow because of the helicopters and drones, which gave the NWO forces with their superior numbers and airpower a feeling of security.

Until Michael and his men made it to the control hub of the tower. Helicopters began falling out of the sky, and now the drones had new targets: anyone wearing a white helmet. The NWO men still alive, despite having an entrenched position and superior weaponry, began throwing down their weapons and surrendering.

The men of the division looked to the tower and saw three bodies in clear NWO leadership regalia being thrown out of the building with a rope attached to them. Above the three dangling bodies of the NWO commanders was a flag from Samson's battle pack that read, "NO QUARTER ASKED, NONE GIVEN" The massacre began.

CHAPTER 12

FALLON

Fallon was confused when he heard the alarm bells ringing but did not see any drones. It was always standard procedure to strafe the enemy with drones if they approached. Fallon realized, though, that the enemy had never attacked before, so this likely led to a lack of respect for the opposing force, something Fallon knew could hurt them greatly.

Having a relatively senior leadership position, Fallon was in charge of four platoons of infantry inside the city. The orders were given from the tower for them to fall back to the city center. This didn't make any sense to Fallon, as the majority of their fortified positions were on the exterior walls and also scattered among the initial mile of interior grounds of the city.

Fallon did as he was ordered and led his men back to form a defensive perimeter around the civilians in the city center. His men were laughing and eager at the opportunity for a fight. Fallon was not. He had been in some battles before with the rebels, and he had taken life, but he had never enjoyed it. It had always been strange to him how other men in his command talked about taking another person's life like it were a game or like there was joy in it. He tried his best not to think about it; he didn't want to begin to dislike or distrust his men. Fallon told himself it was just how they coped with having to kill; everyone coped with it differently.

Fallon heard massive explosions in the direction of the front gate. He didn't want to believe it, but he was certain it had collapsed. These rebels were different, coordinated. This wasn't the fight his men were used to.

Fallon could see the fear in the civilians around him, and he attempted to comfort them as the gunfire rapidly advanced. He ordered his men to get ready, and then thankfully, the air support arrived. His men and the civilians cheered, but Fallon didn't. He knew this meant victory, but it also meant death, too much death, unnecessary death. He might be able to stop his men from killing surrendering men, but he knew the other NWO leadership would encourage the execution of prisoners rather than try to stop it.

Fallon was horrified. He had seen prisoners of war executed before but never this. As the division got nearer, the ground opened up. The civilians he knew and had spoken with were crucified and screaming in agony. He and some of his men went to run out to try to save one until he saw soldiers of the division blowing up as they did the same. Fallon went back to his position, feeling dismayed. His whole world just got flipped. Was he on the wrong side? Was what they did for his family worth this? Could anything ever be worth this?

Before he could gather his thoughts, the NWO aircraft began falling out of the sky. On any other day, he would have been shouting orders and firing at the advancing ground troops because of this, but now he was silent. Fallon almost wanted to lose this battle after what he had just witnessed.

The NWO drones turned on their own and began shooting at his men. His men began firing back, and then the drones stopped, everything stopped, and they were surrounded. Willing to accept any fate given to him after the atrocity he just witnessed, Fallon ordered his men to throw down their weapons and surrender. He wasn't sure what would happen after that until he saw his senior leadership dropped out of the command and control tower hanging. Then he knew his fate and the gunshots he heard, the final thing he heard, were welcome to wash away the screams of the innocent who were crucified.

CHAPTER 13

DAVID

The alarms began sounding this morning, a noise David hadn't heard in a long time and one he forgot what the meaning was. Then Jack told him the terrorists were coming to eat them because they ran out of food and they were cannibals, so they ran to the city center where the bunkers were. They were assured by all the brave soldiers that they had nothing to fear and that the rebel force was small and could never beat a real army.

David asked why they didn't have any planes in the air, and the soldier said they didn't need to waste the fuel. David supposed he knew best. The explosions started, and they were terrifying. It felt like the entire earth was shaking. The soldiers just began laughing, saying how excited they were to finally be able to kill some terrorists.

David was afraid of the thought of being eaten but felt safe surrounded by so many soldiers. He never knew they had so many. The gunfire got closer and closer, and David became more and more scared. Then suddenly, he saw helicopters. He tried to ask the soldier why he needed them now, but the soldier told him to shut up or he'd shoot him.

The gunfire kept creeping closer and closer, and then David saw it. The ground flipped, and the street was covered with women and children crucified. He remembered one older lady; she was that little boy's mother.

The loudspeakers rang out for the good citizens not to be afraid, adding that everyone who was crucified had betrayed them by giving the terrorists information. David thought, "Thank science for that. For a second, I felt bad seeing all these women and children crucified, but if they betrayed us to the cannibal terrorists, then they deserve it!"

The helicopters were falling out of the sky. David knew something was wrong. The soldiers weren't laughing anymore; they looked more terrified than him. The drones were coming toward them and were shooting their own soldiers. David thought something was terribly wrong.

The soldiers had all laid down their weapons. David thought, "They said they would defend us with their lives. Now they're just going to surrender? So we can be eaten? Well, at least the shooting might stop."

David had never seen a dead body up close, and now he was surrounded by them. Thousands upon thousands of NWO white-helmeted soldiers lay dead and dying all around him. If he was afraid before, he was terrified now.

CHAPTER 14

MARY

Mary had gotten her promotion and a husband, Jeff. They were given a beautiful home on the outskirts of the city. She was madly in love with Jeff. He was everything she ever dreamed about, and Jeff told her she was the same. To Mary's surprise Jeff found her journal but didn't tell the experts. They both knew having a journal was a death sentence. It was then she knew this love was real, and she started to believe in things she was told she shouldn't again.

Mary and Jeff were in their home outside the city when the alarms rang out. Mary grabbed Jeff and said they had to get inside the city and to the city center for safety. To her dismay, though, he did not agree with her. Mary then found out why he never turned her in.

Jeff had been secretly sending messages to the Charlamagne Division. He used to be in the military and only hadn't fled the city because he thought the resistance would be futile. When he learned that the division not only thrived but also grew and now had a chance to fight back, he had to help. Mary was so confused. How could this man she loved keep this from her? Then she realized he hadn't. He would try to talk to her often about how things used to be, but she'd always shut him down for fear of what would happen if anyone heard them talking about the past in a good light.

She began thinking about everything they had and how great it was, but then he explained to her it was great because they were together, and they still would be. Mary agreed with Jeff, and they ran in the opposite direction, to the safety of the division.

CHAPTER 15

NATHAN

Nathan's days were all the same now—woke up at 5:00 a.m., reported to work by 5:15 a.m., worked at the steel mill on the campgrounds until noon, took lunch until 12:30 p.m., resumed work until 9:00 p.m., had dinner at 9:30 p.m., and then slept. If anyone produced more material than their quota asked for, they were given another meal break from 5:00 to 5:15 p.m., with a quarter ration extra of food. Their living quarters were just massive barracks with nothing but wooden planks to sleep on. They'd sleep fifty people side by side in three-tiered rows.

One of Nathan's sisters was no longer at this camp. He was told they sent her to a different one now, but he was not told why. No questions were allowed to be asked, and now Nathan had truly learned his lesson. Some of the guards were nice, but most were not. His married sister who was here with her husband would get a half extra ration of food every day, but everyone knew why, and no one envied her or her husband.

Some would whisper about attempting to escape, and then they would see their decapitated heads outside the barracks the following day. Even talk of suicide would get one decapitated, but many talked about it anyway. But with them, they'd make you listen to their screams. They would be tortured for hours before begging to be decapitated.

They couldn't afford to lose their workforce. Everyone wondered why all manual labor jobs were eradicated, but the experts said there was just no need for them anymore. No one knew this was why. No one could know.

CHAPTER 16

PHILLIP

Phillip enjoyed the new title and position he was given, but he did miss combat, or what he called combat. The NWO had strict rules about "wonton" (killing for no reason or due cause) killing of inmates in the camps. They were needed for labor. Phillip relished in the beatings and the few beheadings he got to perform (without the NWO's knowledge, of course), but he missed having free reign.

Phillip took special pleasure in teaching Nathan a lesson about speaking out against the experts. He always had a deep disdain for those who questioned authority, especially when it was an authority he was a part of. Upon arriving the first day at the camp, Phillip requested a synopsis on every inmate so he could pick and choose who to make an example of in front of the others. He decided Nathan was the best target because of his larger family presence there compared with most.

When Phillip first saw Nathan's sister, he knew exactly how to enact this punishment to the outspoken Nathan. He approached Nathan one day at the camp and stated, "I wonder how outspoken your sister will be in my bedchamber." Phillip got just the reaction he wanted; Nathan attempted to strike Phillip, which led to Nathan being tied to a post and whipped for the entire camp to see.

Unlike the last commandant of the prison camp, whenever there was a punishment to be doled out, Phillip stopped all work and made everyone watch. All of Nathan's family members could do nothing but watch as the skin was being torn off his back with every sound of the whip breaking on his back. Nathan's screams were loud at first, but then he locked eyes with his sister, and the screaming was replaced with a steady stream of tears. Phillip knew this meant the physical pain to him was nothing compared with the mental anguish playing in his mind about the horrors his sister would surely face. This was exactly what Phillip wanted to see. Now he could truly enjoy himself in this new role.

Phillip made sure Nathan was still looking at his sister when he sent his guards to grab her and drag her to his building in the center of the camp. She struggled at first with the soldiers, but after a few strikes to the rib cage, she became compliant.

Phillip made her wait inside for a few minutes before entering. He wanted her imagination to run about what was to come. When he entered the room, she was seated at a table in the center of the building with her hands tied to the chair. He pulled out his knife and uncut the ropes. She asked him what his intentions were, and he replied, "I think you know." She looked around the room with tears in her eyes, but then she began undressing.

Phillip had expected and wanted a fight from her, but it did not matter. His excitement from Nathan being whipped in front of her and him knowing what was about to happen was more than enough. Phillip bent her over and was not very pleasant with her. He called her a whore all throughout for not putting up a fight.

When it was over, her face remained the same—expressionless, with tears in her eyes. The first thing she said since asking him his intentions was if she could leave. He replied, "Only after I mark you." Then four soldiers walked in, holding her down, and a fifth one walked in with what appeared to be a metal stick with a glowing red symbol on its end. He said to her, "This is so everyone will know why you will now receive special treatment."

The metal symbol was an NWO with a *P* in the center of it. Phillip had it specially made. All the inmates were branded with the NWO. Phillip did this for any female inmates he wanted to keep for himself. The symbol not only meant they would get extra rations and special treatment, such as more rest time to sleep, more breaks, and so on; it also meant none of the guards could have their way with them. They were Phillip's and his alone.

Phillip received a message from the city of Lexington that the population needed to be eradicated immediately and no trace of the camp left. It was bittersweet for Phillip, as he was just beginning to enjoy his role there. But still, the thought of killing someone at least attempting to fight back did excite him. He sent his trusted man to fetch Nathan's sister one last time.

CHAPTER 17

WILL

The minutemen had a slightly different plan than the rest. Because of their sheer numbers, they figured they'd use this to their advantage. Will had studied WWII well, and he knew that many German victories were won using a pincer method. It was also how the Germans were dealt devastating defeats on both the eastern and western fronts, such as at the Battle of Kursk and the Battle of the Bulge on the West.

Will also knew the NWO leaders not only had no respect for any rebel group, but they also had ardent disdain for them. Even if they had intelligence reports telling them about the numbers of Will's force, they would not believe it.

So the plan was simple. Instead of a frontal assault with simultaneous small attacks on access points, they would hit the access points first with small fast-moving vehicles. The vehicles would then flee directly north, hopefully drawing out a large contingent of the NWO force that would subsequently be surrounded and decimated.

This plan worked like a charm initially, much to Will's surprise. The NWO hadn't even scrambled any aircraft; they simply sent out a fully armored division and two infantry divisions. Once they were approximately ten miles north of the city, far enough away for reinforcements to take time but close enough for their radios to still transmit for reinforcements, they were absolutely surrounded.

This was where the minutemen differed from the Charlamagne Division—they offered quarter, and they meant it. But it was also where the northeast NWO differed from the southern NWO—they didn't take it. Even though the NWO personnel were surrounded, they were able to inflict a large number of casualties on the minutemen simply because of strength of their vehicles and their superior weaponry.

But the minutemen's plan wasn't just to massacre them; it was to capture their tanks, and now they had an entire tank division at their disposal. Because of guerrilla tactics and "sticky bombs" that disabled the tanks tracks, they could force the tank personnel to surrender or flush them out with smaller munitions that would leave the tank operable. As a result, the minutemen were able to capture most of the armored fighting vehicles.

Now there was a force double the size coming at the minutemen; this battle would be different. The battle raged on, with Will in the lead captured tank for the minutemen. Their tanks were outnumbered 3–1, but the minutemen infantry outnumbered the NWO infantry 7–1. Tank shells and artillery rounds from the NWO main guns fell everywhere.

The minutemen began winning the battle. They could see the NWO numbers dwindling, and even some of them started to flee. Then they heard it. An NWO bomber whizzed by, dropping a devastating payload. Now Will saw his own lines started to break as helicopters, drones, and bombers covered the sky.

Many of the minutemen began to flee. Will tried hard shouting at them to hold the line and continue the fight, but it seemed futile. He knew this attack was a huge risk, but they were having such success. He didn't want all that to be wasted, nor did he want the lives that they had lost to be for naught. The tank he was in was still dealing devastating damage, but it couldn't move. He and his men knew they would likely die in this spot. While it seemed like most of the minutemen were fleeing, there were still thousands following orders and continuing the fight. Will was proud to die alongside them.

Miraculously, the planes and helicopters began falling, and the drones turned on the NWO soldiers. The fleeing minutemen saw this and turned back and were now pushing toward the front. Will did not know what was happening, but he did not care. He ordered all the minutemen to charge the city, for they now had an overwhelming advantage.

Maybe because of what Phillip had done or maybe just because of how the Northeast was wired, contrastingly to Lexington where all the people were inside the city center fleeing from the rebels. Here, thousands were coming outside, grabbing weapons, and joining the fight.

Will saw where the command and control room tower was, and he ordered all his special operators into it with him. While his men cleared the city, already having an overwhelming infantry advantage, but now also having the superior vehicles, airpower, and support of the city, they took control quickly. When he arrived at the tower, there was a message on repeat: "We have captured Lexington and are now controlling all NWO drones in North America. Establish communication lines. The war has finally begun".

CHAPTER 18

MICHAEL

Michael hadn't planned on executing the NWO leadership inside that room. He knew he shouldn't have, and he knew Samson wouldn't have. They could have given him valuable information. But his rage consumed him. Now he was confounded by the last outgoing message. It stated, "Eradicate the population. Leave no trace of the camp."

Michael knew the experts spoke of the rebels being in camps, but there was no way they were near the Charlamagne camp. He sent word to Jeff. If anyone would know, Jeff would.

Jeff arrived at the city center shortly after. Michael was quick and asked him about a camp nearby. Jeff looked terrified. All Jeff heard was rumors, but he didn't believe them. He knew the NWO was bad but, surely, not that bad. Michael finally got it out of Jeff, the rumors at least. Now Michael had a new mission for his men.

Not more than twenty miles west of the city, they found it. They might not have found it if not for the smell. The smell of dead bodies was one you could never forget once you smelled it. But the smell of thousands, you could never get rid of.

They tried to approach stealthily, but machine-gun fire erupted on their position, pinning Michael and his men in place. He had seen the two towers but hadn't seen any movement from them, so he assumed they were unmanned. A mistake Samson wouldn't have made, he thought as he and his men took cover. While attempting to move to a better position in the tree line just behind them, one of the towers exploded. Michael and his men were confused; they were the only division members who even knew of this place. Shortly after that the other tower was no longer firing, and the gate began to open.

As they approached there were a few people left, standing by the fences, which were covered in concertina wire. They clearly hadn't been fed in weeks. There were massive piles of dead bodies. They saw to the northeast corner of the camp what looked to be the most well-kept building in the camp. If there was a commander there, that was where he'd be.

They entered the building and found it completely empty, aside from a naked woman sobbing and holding on to a fork. She wouldn't speak to anyone, just kept rocking back and forth, asking for Nathan.

Suddenly, a man clad in half prisoner clothes and half body armor appeared, armed with a pistol. At first Michael drew his weapon on him, then noticed the clothing and began asking who he was. The man said his name was Nathan, and the woman in the corner was his sister. Nathan began telling Michael everything.

Michael and his men were always told they were fighting a war of good versus evil, and they all believed it. But now they had truly seen the evil they were fighting. Now their resolve was greater than ever.

Michael ordered all survivors sent to the division doctors and given food, water, and clothes. They had taken the city, but they would not stay there. Even if they won every battle in North America on this day, the NWO army would be back. Their only hope was to go back to where their division had lived for years and continue the war from there for now.

CHAPTER 19

PHILLIP

When Nathan's sister arrived, Phillip's orders had already been dispatched. Everyone was to be slaughtered, except Nathan's family. They were to be brought to Phillip's quarters in five minutes.

Nathan's sister knew her duty, and so she undressed and got ready. Phillip began taking her as he always had, only this time he placed handcuffs on her and left her hands in the front so her family would see them. She thought it was strange but knew questioning it wouldn't do her any good. Then the door opened, and fear flushed over her. In walked two camp guards, then her husband, her daughter, Nathan, and her other brother flanked by two more camp guards following them.

Nathan's sister now began to scream and fight, which caused Phillip to strike her. When he did so, Nathan and his brother attempted to fight as well but were overwhelmed. Suddenly, an alarm rang out. Phillip stopped and looked curious for a moment, and then the alarm bell rang again. He ordered his men outside to fight off the terrorists, and he began putting on his gear.

Then Phillip felt a sharp pain in his neck and a cool liquid running down onto his chest. He turned and saw Nathan's sister had stabbed him in the jugular. Nathan, his brother, and her husband quickly ran over to continue stabbing him repeatedly, listening to the gurgling sounds he made as he took his last agonizing breaths. They then grabbed his pistol, rifle, and armor and suited up themselves. They hid his body in case they lost the fight and told her to remain inside the building, and they began engaging the NWO troops from behind.

CHAPTER 20

D A V I D

David's fear was palpable. He saw men and women coming toward him and couldn't picture them as anything but demons. He began having auditory exclusion due to his fear. He saw them and knew they were speaking to him but couldn't hear anything. Everything went black.

David woke up in a hospital. He felt relieved thinking it must have all been a dream. If they had actually lost and he was captured by the terrorists, they'd be feasting on his flesh right now, not caring for him in a hospital. His relief faded away when he saw other civilians on the hospital beds around him, and also men and women dressed in combat gear, with the funny hats that the Charlamagne Division wore.

His fear was coming back. He thought, "Are they just keeping me alive so they can eat me later? What is going on?" Finally, a nurse came over and asked him how he was feeling. He stuttered. He had never stuttered before, but he was so terrified. He asked her who won the battle, and she said, "The division did. Thank God, we're all saved." Everything went black again.

David woke back up, but now his memory was clear. The nurse saw he was waking up again and said, "You're not going to pass out again, are you? I know there's a lot of excitement about being liberated, but you're the first I've seen be that excited." David thought, "Excited?" He was so confused. "People are excited that the terrorists won? Who? Why?" David didn't know what to say, so he just asked how long she had been a nurse for. He was shocked when she said two years. He knew there were no new nursing licenses being given out since the experts took over all medicine, and the need for hospitals plummeted. They were only now used by the NWO military during emergencies.

He asked where she got her license from, and she laughed and said, "They don't give a fancy license in the division. But you're taught by some of the best." David couldn't understand it. "Why have nurses, and especially ones working on people you mean to eat? It doesn't make sense," he thought.

David was told his recovery was going to take a few days since he got a gash in his skull when he passed out on the cement. His roommates were on their way to see him, though. David began freaking out, stating it couldn't be. Before the hospitals went away, they were very strict about no visitors, and it should be kept that way. The nurse assured him all would be fine, and they always allowed visitors at hospitals in the division. No one had died yet from seeing a friendly face.

CHAPTER 21

MARY

Mary arrived at the division grounds before Jeff. She was greeted like a long-lost friend, as were all the newly liberated civilians from Lexington. Mary was confused by this. She agreed to go with Jeff but was scared because of what she was told about these people. No one had fangs, there were no children being burned, and everyone was very nice to her.

A woman dressed like a nurse named Janet took Mary and a few others around the grounds, then promptly showed them to their homes. Mary was surprised that everyone had their own home in this new world. This home was neither as big nor as nice as what she and Jeff had previously, but it was better than she was expecting.

The homes everyone was given in the division were two-story homes, approximately 1,800 square feet, with three bedrooms and two bathrooms. Every family got one. Single people were given a home that was 1,200 square feet, with two bedrooms and one bathroom. The division, while initially comprised largely of military members, saw its ranks swell with many former laborers during the initial flee from the city. Because of this, their skill sets in construction were unmatched by the other rebel divisions. The homes were made of whatever materials were at hand. Because of the abundance of trees that littered the mountainside, where they spent time hiding from the drones, the majority of them were made of wood.

Mary was surprised to find the home had a beautiful interior, exactly as she would have made her own home look if she had been allowed any decorative abilities in the home the experts gave her. The kitchen had no walls separating it from the other rooms, the floors were all bare wood, with natural light emanating from windows all around the home. The living/dining room had a massive table in the center, with two large benches on either side. There was a magnificent fireplace, and more books than she could have ever dreamed of reading.

When Jeff arrived she explained how perfect the house was and how she loved how the division designed their homes as opposed to how the experts did. Jeff then told her the designs were done per the residents' requests. She was stunned, but it all made sense. She had always whispered to Jeff about how she wished their home could look, and now it was exactly that, down to the last detail. She was overcome with a feeling of gratitude that she had found a love that was secretly building her a dream home, in a time like this. The books were his touch. He was always reading, but these books here wouldn't be allowed in their old world; the experts had outlawed most of them.

Jeff knew Mary would have a lot of questions, but his in-depth intelligence reports were needed. He answered as many as he could before leaving for the division's headquarters, located 200 feet underneath the largest of the three mountains that surrounded their camp. He asked Mary if she would like to go with him and meet the leaders of their new world. Mary was still in shock and largely afraid of everything. The last thing she wanted was to be away from Jeff, so she went with him, into the mountain.

CHAPTER 22

NATHAN

Nathan was told to follow one of the guards. This was not unusual, but the smirk on the guard's face was. To Nathan's surprise he saw his other brother and his sister's husband with their daughter also being led by guards over to him. This was unusual; they forbid members of the same family congregating during daytime. That was why they gave all of them different work purposes.

Nathan, his brother, and his sister's husband clutching his daughter were all walked to the main headquarters of the camp flanked by four guards. Nathan was confused and scared. He didn't think they meant to kill him because he knew they needed the labor, but it couldn't be good wherever he was being led to.

When they reach the headquarters door, the guard who smirked at Nathan said, "Now you all get to see why that whore gets extra food." The door opened, and rage set over Nathan as he saw what Phillip was doing to his sister. He saw her fighting too, but it was futile. Nathan attempted to overwhelm the guards as did his brother and her husband, but they had been malnourished for months, and they did not have the strength for this fight. They shielded the daughter's eyes but she could still hear the grunting and the actions of what was happening with her mother and Phillip.

Then the alarm sounded. Phillip stopped what he was doing and began issuing orders to his men. The guards all started running toward the front gates. Nathan, his brother, and his sister's husband now saw an opportunity and they took it.

They would have killed Phillip given the opportunity for a litany of reasons, but now they wanted him to suffer. That was why when Nathan's sister stabbed Phillip in the jugular, a death they all believed would be too quick, Nathan and the rest began stabbing him repeatedly, ensuring every last breath of Phillip would be taken with as much pain as possible.

Nathan and his comrades then told his sister to hide, but they began gearing up. Phillip might be dead, but they did not know the size of the force sent to liberate them, and they would do anything they could to make sure they succeeded. They grabbed Phillip's armor, pistol, and rifle, as well as some grenades Phillip had on his vest. They made for the gate and the two machine gun towers next to it.

They could hear the towers' machine guns talking loudly, almost in sync with each other. When one gun burst, the other was quiet, then when the quiet one burst, the former became quiet. Nathan could see that the force coming to liberate them was a small contingent of infantry, so he rushed toward the north machine gun tower. Nathan's brother rushed to the south with grenades in hand. He reached the south tower before Nathan reached the north. He lobbed his grenades up from below and watched as a ferocious explosion killed the three men inside the south tower.

Nathan was climbing the north tower now, pistol in hand, while his brother-in-law was standing at the base with his rifle, defending his ascent. Nathan made it to the tower and was quickly able to deliver three rounds to the backs of the heads of the unsuspecting machine gunners nested in the north tower. The way was now clear for the liberators.

Nathan was unsure who these men were and what they would do. For all he knew, they could be an NWO team sent in to clear them out, including the guards. So he and his comrades quickly moved back to the headquarters where their sister was, but they took up a position to watch these men, hoping they were liberators, as they moved through the camp.

It was quickly evident to Nathan that these men were not here to cause harm and that they were, in fact, here as liberators. When he saw one of them enter the headquarters where his sister was, he followed in behind.

CHAPTER 23

BRUSSELS

Word reached the secretary-general of the NWO, Bolton, that Lexington and Boston had fallen, Dallas was on the brink, and other US cities were being attacked. Bolton called for an emergency meeting of all NWO leadership.

Generals Rumsfeld of the Eastern colonies, Chadwik of the African colonies, Kim of the Asian colonies, Ruiz of the South American colonies, and Dietrich of the Western European colonies were all in attendance. All that was missing was the general of the North American colonies, Yelden, who was at Lexington and was presumed dead or captured.

Bolton's first order of business was that word of this could never reach anywhere outside the colonies affected. The order was given to cut off all of North America from communication lines with the rest of the world. Ruiz and Dietrich gave ardent protest to this, largely because only two colonies had definitely fallen, and they needed to know if reinforcements were needed at the other seventeen. It fell on deaf ears.

Bolton stated it mattered not if every North American colony fell, then they would make them a nuclear wasteland, never to be inhabited again. He said, "We don't need them. They need us." Ruiz asked for permission to send his military in to assist in Dallas and any other colonies they could. Bolton denied this request, as there was no way to know for certain they had not sent out communication already to other parts of the world since Lexington was a communications and command and control hub for all of North America.

Bolton ordered all military forces for the NWO to be placed on high alert and for thirty-three out of the total thirty-eight bomber squadrons to be sent to Dietrich and Ruiz's command to be utilized to annihilate the North Americans left living. This order was met with opposition from Ruiz and Chadwik, who stated they had large civilian populations in the North American colonies, and wiping them out would not be good for overall work production.

Bolton did not care. He was always a man out solely for his own ambition. Bolton was one of few European generals to become a millionaire on a government salary and the only one to become a billionaire. No one knew how until the war broke out, and now no one would dare state how publicly.

They said everyone was equal in this new world, but men like Bolton didn't live in a house on the outskirts of the city. They had multiple waterfront mansions all across the world. They had private planes with their own fighter jet escorts to ferry them around to these mansions, them and whoever they chose to bring as guests. The world was only equal to those not in the club, and even then "equal" was a loose term.

Dietrich was surprisingly quiet upon being told to level North America. He was always known as a sentimental man, and this was seen to stall his career advancement in the NWO. Somehow he achieved the position he did, but nevertheless, his acceptance of the order was curious to Ruiz.

After the meeting adjourned, Ruiz asked Dietrich why, and Dietrich explained that as the general of the Western European colonies, he already had the most formidable navy and tank forces. Now he would also have the largest fleet of aircraft. With Yelden out of the game and with that potentially the production power of the Americas, the only general with any advantage over him was Rumsfeld, given the sheer size of the Eastern European infantry and the landscape that had thwarted many superior forces throughout history.

Dietrich had never been a very ambitious man; he did his duty and showed too much compassion to the enemy everyone agreed, so this was strange to Ruiz. He asked Dietrich if he would fulfill his duty and use the bombers as he was told, to which Dietrich replied, "Of course. Our allegiance is to the order, and to the order is our allegiance." Ruiz did not trust the way Dietrich said it, so he made his own plans.

CHAPTER 24

MICHAEL

It was urgent that the word got out as quickly as possible about the success of the mission. Michael started to think he might have made a mistake for liberating that camp before sending out a message to Europe and the other continents, but in the end he realized that camp's liberation was more important. Now he could also tell the world what the NWO was truly up to.

Michael headed back to the control tower and was relieved to find out that the other rebel groups in the United States had received his first message. He also learned that Dallas had been taken, along with Boston, New Orleans, Durham, and Charleston. Los Angeles had been a terribly bloody defeat for the rebel forces, as were DC, Manhattan, and Seattle. There was still no word from the other cities.

Michael's joy for the victory was quickly washed away by his grief for the rebels of his own division and of many others who perished on that day. He knew the only way their deaths would have meaning was if they won this war, and so win it they must.

Michael attempted to send out a message to every continent about their victories and about the camps, but it wouldn't send. The communication lines to the outside world had been cut. Regardless, he could still get messages to the other cities in North America, and so he did. He sent out messages for all divisions to come together. He used an encrypted code they had been using to communicate. It was a mix of four old native American tribal languages, something the NWO leadership couldn't decipher if they intercepted. He ordered them to destroy the cities they had captured and meet him in the mountains.

Another message was sent to all the inhabitants inside the cities under NWO control. Every command and control tower had the ability to transmit emergency messages to every television set in every home inside their city. The Lexington tower could also send a message to every other city in North America.

The message reads, "To all those living under the tyranny of the so-called experts, to all those living under the tyranny of the NWO, you do have a choice. We have taken major cities across the continent today, and if you're receiving this message, you heard the alarms in your own city. Brave men and women died outside your walls trying to liberate you. Do not believe the lies. We live lives rooted in faith and family, we are not here to harm any, but we are here to free all. If you enjoy living without ownership of your own lives, if you enjoy living in slavery, only being allowed to do what the experts say when they say, then I suggest you flee for Europe or South America. Our forces may not have liberated your city today, we may not be there tomorrow, but soon every city in America will be free again. Join us."

CHAPTER 25

MARY

Mary was astonished by the structures built hundreds of feet underground. She was also overwhelmed by how close people were willing to get to each other to speak and seeing that people were speaking in groups of more than two people at a time. Everywhere she went she was greeted with hugs, which she was reluctant to accept at first, but now she couldn't help but feel something nice about human contact again.

After taking an elevator down, Mary and Jeff boarded a train system and were on the train for what had to be three minutes. Mary could not comprehend how massive these tunnels must be. The trains were unlike any she had ever seen before; there were no electrical rails and no wheels on the train. The train itself appeared to just float above the ground while traveling at a high rate of speed. Jeff tried explaining to her that the train ran on high-powered positive and negative magnets constantly interacting from lateral and horizontal directions, but this was all too much to her at once, and she was just happy to be with him to help her through it all.

They arrived at the headquarters, which was unbecoming to look at, unlike the military structures of the NWO. Unlike the beautifully decorated home she now lived in, this structure and the rooms within had nothing that didn't serve a purpose. There was no pomp or mahogany couches, just desks, chairs, and communications apparatuses, which until the capture of Lexington were nothing more than relics to look at.

To Mary's surprise Jeff was greeted with hugs and smiles, as if everyone inside there knew him well. Her intuition was correct—Jeff was an avid hunter she had always believed, and the NWO, while not allowing regular citizens to eat meat, would allow those who lived in the homes on the outskirts to go hunting and eat whatever they could find. Mary always wondered if Jeff just wasn't good at hunting because he rarely brought meat home, but now she learned he was meeting with these senior leaders every time to dispatch messages.

Mary was introduced to the division's top generals—General Roosevelt, General Dondarion, and Division Leader Spear. They all greeted Mary with hugs and thanked her for her service to the division and for trusting Jeff to come with him all this way. Mary was given free rein to walk around the headquarters while Jeff and the leadership of the division talked about all the intel Jeff had compiled.

Mary exited the headquarters to take a walk around the underground complex and saw what looked like a park. She walked over, and there were children playing, trees as green as those above ground, swing sets, and a jungle gym. Mary was clearly perplexed. Another woman named Monica approached her. Monica said she had seen the perplexed looked many times over the past five years, as she was one of the first to leave with the division and always spotted a newcomer.

Monica began to explain how they were able to create an almost identical atmosphere to the aboveground world hundreds of feet below ground. She said it was in case the NWO found their location and decided to use their bombers on the division. They could sustain the entire population down there, with enough natural vegetation being grown, oxygen, and meat supplies to last them two decades. Mary was overwhelmed; she didn't know what to think. She asked about the meat, some things she realized she was lied to about. "But meat, meat has always been bad for you," she proclaimed. Monica laughed and said she hadn't eaten anything but meat for the past five years, and she had never felt better. Mary didn't know what to believe anymore.

Jeff returned, took Mary's hand, and they began walking back to the train to take them to the surface. Jeff apologized to Mary for keeping all this a secret from her for so long but said he had to protect her. It was probably the only thing Mary had learned today that she understood. They returned to their home, and Jeff explained everything.

CHAPTER 26

RUIZ

Ruiz was uneasy about Dietrich's comments, so he sought out Bolton and told him that he didn't think Dietrich should be given so many assets. Bolton, being a man born in Western Europe, didn't much like what this darker-skinned South American comrade was trying to insinuate about one of his top men. Bolton and Dietrich had served together in the same unit for the Germans before the NWO began. Bolton dismissed Ruiz's insinuations and told him never to question his authority again.

Ruiz returned to South America and put his military on full alert as ordered, but he also ordered a standby for his naval forces without Bolton's order. Ruiz meant to bomb North America as ordered but then prepared to wage a naval war against Dietrich if necessary. Dietrich might have inherited the largest fleet, with the most aircraft carriers, but the South American navy had lethal submarines, and these submarines knew how to evade NWO sonar systems.

Without permission to do so, Ruiz ordered his subs to depart for the East Atlantic Ocean and standby there for further orders. He had two days before the bombing began, and he wanted his subs in place in case Dietrich decided to betray the NWO.

To Ruiz's surprise, of the thirty-three bomber squadrons, he was given nineteen. The East Coast had much more populous colonies, and Lexington had strong AA defensive weapons. Ruiz knew what this meant; his advice did not fall on deaf ears. Ruiz now put his ground forces on full mobilization. If Dietrich did betray them, Ruiz's ground forces would have a distinct edge in a ground conflict in North America.

The day had arrived. Ruiz ordered eight of his nineteen squadrons to level the West Coast and turn it into a nuclear wasteland. Within hours, he received word that all targets were hit, with not a single plane lost. Ruiz didn't wait for word from Dietrich about the success of his mission. He ordered his remaining eleven squadrons to the East Coast and his navy to engage any military vessel they saw.

CHAPTER 27

WILL

Will received the Charlamagne Division's last message and ordered the minutemen to gather all civilians and all supplies and weapons they could and head for the rendezvous point with the division. The minutemen were ecstatic after such a victory, one that few, if any, truly saw coming. Luckily, they were able to grab some antiair weapons, as airpower was the main thing they feared.

It took about two days, but finally, they felt they had enough provisions to last them the journey to the rendezvous. Will had spent much of these two days trying to comfort the few civilians who wished to remain under the yolk of the NWO. Anyone who wished to remain in the city was allowed to, but they did their best to convince them otherwise. Despite this, a couple of thousand still remained behind, trusting that the NWO would send a new army and new experts for them to follow.

Will's men wanted him to force them to come along, saying they knew too much about the minutemen's size and capabilities. But Will refused, stating, "We cannot call ourselves freedom fighters if we do not allow others the freedom to choose for themselves."

Will and the minutemen were approximately seventy-five miles outside the city when they heard it, a loud explosion, and then they all saw a massive mushroom cloud. They couldn't believe it. They had heard reports about the work camps, but they were murdering people who wished to remain loyal to them. Will ordered all civilians to push toward the rendezvous and all willing to fight to grab weapons. They did not have enough AA weapons for everyone; in reality they only had captured roughly two dozen, but it did not matter. Hope was something these newly freed civilians hadn't felt in two years or more. He wasn't going to deprive them of it now.

Planes began converging from the southwest and the east. The ones from the east gave an easier shot for the AA weapons, so Will ordered his batteries to focus on them. Three direct hits and three planes fell out of the sky. The men cheered, until a bomb from one of the planes from the southwest and ripped the front of the convoy, where it was all civilians.

Then bewildering to all who saw, the NWO planes from the east began engaging the planes from the southwest. The eastern planes were shooting down the bombers approaching from the southwest. Will was unsure if they were truly friendly, but he knew it was the only chance his people had. He ordered all his men to fire only on planes from the southwest. Within minutes all bombers approaching from the southwest were destroyed.

Will and his men cheered again, but it didn't last long. Mechanized units were heard approaching. They took cover as best they could, but the convoy was too big to truly take cover and hide. There was something different about these tanks. The typical NWO tank had an active camouflage system, so it could be heard but couldn't be seen, and if one was close enough to see it, it was painted bright white. These tanks were painted in the old camouflage of the US military.

Will again didn't know what to believe, but he broke his cover and went out to meet whoever was leading these troops.

Will was met by a man named Colonel Anderson. Colonel Anderson told him that they were with the Western European contingent of the NWO, but they had essentially mutinied. Their air force would support all that they could to make it to link up with the other survivors, and Colonel Anderson's mechanized brigade along with three others were sent there the day of the uprisings to assist against any ground invasion.

Will was beside himself. He was a big man, and his men had never seen tears in his eyes, but now he couldn't help it. They might actually win the war.

CHAPTER 28

DIETRICH

After the meeting concluded, Dietrich headed straight to his headquarters. Many would fear spies, or rats doing what he was about to do, but he didn't. Most of his men were US, UK, French, or German military. They joined because they did not feel there was any legitimate chance of a resistance. Lexington, Boston, Dallas, and the others showed them otherwise.

Dietrich told his top generals his plan. In the room were Admiral Copeland, General Winters, and General Carter. The admiral was to keep the fleet close to the coastlines. He knew when his first shots were fired, the entire NWO would come after them, and against the coastlines they had the combined force of their navy and their mechanized units. General Winters was to mobilize all his men to the border with the Eastern European contingent and be prepared for a first strike on a moment's notice. General Carter would oversee the defense from the south and the west of Western Europe.

Missing from this was Colonel Anderson, whom Dietrich now told the men he was already sent with three armor brigades to the Canadian territories to assist the rebels. The bombers Bolton gave him would stay in Western Europe, but half his fighter aircraft were sent with Colonel Anderson. He explained to the rest of the men in the room that they all knew what they were undertaking when they spoke of this. But now it was real, and chances were, this would not end in their favor. It would likely end with their entire families being mutilated in front of them and then a long existence of torture. Dietrich was proud to see his men's faces didn't change at these words; they knew the cost, they knew the risk, and they would make the same decision anyway.

Dietrich told Winters when the first plane was shot down over the Americas, he was to make for the Eastern European headquarters with all haste. If they could cut the head off the snake, it would disrupt the counteroffensives launched from the African, Asian, and South American contingents. Once the Eastern European headquarters had been secured, the navy would be sent to attack South America, with the help of the rebel forces from the north and Colonel Anderson's brigades, as well as the bombers. They did not wish to level entire colonies, but they would if they needed to.

CHAPTER 29

THE NIGHT BEFORE

The night before the battle was to begin, Colonel Anderson visited with the fighter pilots. He had them all fall in and explained to them that he understood if any man wished to not take part in this mission, if anyone wished to sail back to Europe, he would allow it. He explained that they would be flying to shoot down aircraft flown by people they might have trained with to protect the people who would likely be shooting at them. Some of them might be killed by the very people they were attempting to protect. He asked them to think of their oaths to their national militaries before they gave an oath to the NWO. He asked them to remember the sense of camaraderie they once had and the feeling they once had fighting to protect rather than to enslave.

He told them to think of their own families, who were forced into this world. If they said anything that was not accepted or ate an apple they grew themselves, they would be publicly hanged. He asked if they did not deserve a better world, a free world. The pilots erupted in cheer; not a single one asked to be sent home.

Colonel Anderson ordered all his tanks to be painted how they were when they fought for their nations. His brigade was composed of men from many different nations, but whichever nation was most represented in any mechanized unit, that was the pattern it would be painted in. The men were jubilant at that, as he knew they would be. They hadn't fought for a cause they truly believed in in a long time. He hadn't either, and he, too, forgot what it felt like. But now he was remembering what he learned in history and in combat himself. Fighting for the right cause could turn the tide in any battle because there was no fear in dying for the right cause, and fear could be spread among an adversary like a lethal virus.

Colonel Anderson now took time to sit down. True rest wouldn't come for him tonight; it never had the night before a battle. This battle very well might be his last. He knew even if he and his men succeeded tomorrow, there was still little chance of victory. It did not matter. The colonel lost two of his daughters to the vaccine, his wife to the virus, and his son was believed to be missing. He stayed in the military for the health care and steady pay to provide for his family. Without having to worry about retribution against them, he felt he could start making different choices, the right choices.

CHAPTER 30

BOLTON

Word reached Bolton fast from the happenings in North America. Ruiz had anticipated some sort of betrayal by Dietrich, but not this bold. Bolton almost looked relieved when word reached him, but he acted steadfastly. He ordered all NWO contingents to mobilize their ground forces to Eastern Europe so they could steamroll Dietrich and his men. He accepted Ruiz's request to keep his ground forces in South America and march them north to annihilate any survivors from the rebels.

The last thing Bolton wanted was word getting out of a rebel uprising that not only had victories but now also had the support of an entire contingent of NWO military power. He despised the common folk and did not respect them in combat, but nevertheless, he wanted them alive so they could perform the necessary tasks for the NWO to keep him in power.

Bolton ordered all remaining bomber squadrons to be sent to the westernmost border of the Eastern European lands. He meant to annihilate not just Dietrich but all who lived under him. Before leaving his command center, he made a final order to activate the Felix legions.

The Felix legions were composed of the top mercenary groups from before the NWO existed. They were all the top special forces soldiers from every nation who made millions of dollars simply killing for hire. When the NWO took over, they announced they were outlawing mercenary groups, and the people cheered. But it was a rouse; all the mercenary groups were simply placed under new management.

The Felix legions gained notoriety in their handling of the Berlin uprising to the NWO. When the Felix legions were sent in, they began a mass campaign of torture and murder on anyone who *might* have information on any rebel. If a rebel had a family, he could rest assured every member of that family, including cousins and distant relatives, would be tortured and killed—in the most gruesome ways imaginable. They took techniques from the Bolshevik uprising over the czar in Russia. They would tie someone to a post in the middle of the town square, cut a hole in them, and pull out their small intestines, then nail the small intestines to the post. They would then make the tortured person run in circles around the tree until all their intestines had fallen out. Everyone in Berlin and everyone under NWO occupation in the Eastern European territories knew of the Felix legions, and most who remained in Berlin and the east knew someone butchered by them.

Since the NWO had complete control of all sources of information, outside the Eastern European contingent, little was known of the Felix legions, aside from them being Bolton's most favored military unit. He gave them the top equipment the NWO had to offer—tanks that were virtually invisible even to radar systems, armor that was cheap and resistant to almost any rifle round, even helicopters that could go undetected by sight and radar while carrying a payload capable of leveling an entire colony.

The Felix legions were rarely used by the NWO because of their lack of following any command structure. Bolton always referred to them as his wild dogs; once he let them off their leash, it wasn't easy to get them back on it.

Bolton didn't need them back on their leash, though; he needed this rebellion crushed and immediately, and he did not care who died along the way. Or how they died.

Bolton went to his chambers where his wife awaited him. He couldn't wait to tell her about the smile on his face, but she knew. She knew that smile. She hadn't seen that smile since he last came back from combat. She knew his happiness came from one thing, and one thing only: killing. Bolton told her how relieved he was to finally have an actual opponent in the field as opposed to the despicable people who just put their hands out and asked for what others earned.

Bolton's wife, Nancy, never liked the bloodshed, never liked any of what it was that made her husband happy. But she loved her status, she loved the life his wicked ways afforded them, and she loved having all her children go to the top school in the entire world just because of who their father was. For this, his sociopathic murderous tendencies were an easy trade-off.

Bolton packed a few bags and told her he would be back soon, as this war wouldn't last long.

CHAPTER 31

WINTERS

At 6:00 a.m. on June 17, 2035, the order was given. Winters had an eerie feeling. He felt akin to many before him—Napolean, the field marshals of the Wehrmacht, the Prussian generals. He knew this assault would be different than theirs. This wasn't a war of occupation but a war of liberation. This wasn't a battle to bring a populace under a new flag; it was one to free it from its rulers and kill its rulers given the chance.

Within six hours of the order, the entirety of the force was 200 miles inside the eastern territories meeting with minimal resistance. Every city they approached welcomed them as liberators and freely gave information on the happenings of the NWO military in the eastern block. This was shocking to the entire command staff; NWO civilian populations usually were not this easy to liberate because of a great deal of brainwashing.

At 2:45 p.m., Winters reported to Dietrich their first heavy contact of the day. Dietrich was also surprised at the success. By this time they were 360 miles east, and at this rate they would be closing on the capital within a day. Winter's overwhelming tank superiority quickly crushed the resistance, and he found himself with over two hundred thousand men surrendering. A tough decision must be made, tough but necessary. This force had a clear mission in mind, and they couldn't waste manpower housing, guarding, or valuable resources feeding prisoners. They knew what would happen to them if they get caught, so they must do the same. They offered to anyone who would join their cause one opportunity to do so, and a transport would take them to the western stronghold of England, where they would be trained and watched. Anyone who refused would die on this day.

Word reached Winters that Bolton had ordered all the Africa and Asia ground forces to be mobilized in Eastern Europe. Time was running out. This could turn into a huge blunder for Bolton if Winters was successful in capturing the capital before those troops arrived. They would have options: fortify their position and do devastating damage to the other continental forces or perform a tactical retreat with special operators conducting rear guard strikes against advancing columns to slow the enemy's advance while they reached their fortified positions in the west.

Winters did not wish to get ahead of himself; he had to win the battle today before he spent too much time thinking on tomorrow's battle. But the thought was good. He decided to send a small group of his men to clear out all the liberated cities and begin marching them west to safety. They came as liberators, and he knew the price these people would pay for assisting him and his men.

The attack proceeded on with lightning speeds. Small skirmishes were happening on the way, but they were becoming within one hundred miles of the capital. They took the Eastern Europeans completely off guard. Many of their mechanized and artillery corps and aircraft were still on board freights heading west when the attack began, which made Winters wonder. If they had not known about their attack east, why were they mobilizing in the west?

He had no time to ponder on this, though. The mission was succeeding but had not been successful yet, and it needed to be. The fate of the entire war hung on the success of this mission.

The western armies reach fifty miles outside the capital, and all hell broke loose. It was as if every artillery gun in the world was on them at once. Western tanks were resilient to artillery blasts, thanks to an ingenious new leopard tank designed by the Germans. But a direct hit would still destroy the tank and its crew.

Winters requested Dietrich to allow for a slowdown so his men could hunker down and wait out the barrage, which would also allow for the slower units, the infantry, and the heavier tanks/artillery a chance to catch up. Dietrich denied this request, ordering the smaller and more mobile mechanized units to flank around the city, taking out any artillery positions in their path, while the heavy tanks were instructed to pick up the pace and steamroll straight into the capital.

Winters did not like this order, but as a good soldier, he followed it. Within hours his losses were immense, the smaller tanks were getting shredded by entrenched antitank guns, but they persisted on. Battle after battle raged all around the city while Winters watched on helplessly, waiting and praying for the heavy tanks to arrive.

Just as the pincer was about to close around the city, Winters saw a battalion all in black approaching from the north. He knew who that was; it was one of the Felix legions. The small mechanized units on the northern side of the city were cut into two like a hot knife through butter. The mechanized units to the east side of the city were now cut off from the rest.

The Felix legions left them and began their drive straight at Winters's forward line. Thankfully for Winters, as good as the legions' tanks were, their crews were not nearly as well trained as a western tank crew. This advantage was not to be overlooked. The Felix tanks had a cloaking system embedded in them, making their initial contact a massive surprise. But Dietrich knew of the tanks' cloaking systems and was able to have his engineers create a new radar system that could make them visible to his tank crews.

The western tanks began engaging the Felix tanks. The battle was going well until rockets just started dropping from thin air. Winters had heard about invisible helicopters but didn't believe they actually existed. He quickly sent word to Dietrich.

The more agile tanks of the western armies were being cut to shreds now, and Winters's army was starting to look more like a graveyard. The mightiest of all the armies in the world at the moment was being torn up by a group of mercenaries. It was unthinkable.

The heavies and artillery began arriving, accompanied by their AA tanks. Winters ordered all artillery to fire flares over the battlefield. It was a shot in the dark, but he believed with the illumination of a flare, maybe the stealth coating would produce a glare, and if a well-trained eye could see it, they could shoot it.

A massive barrage of flares rang out and illuminated the daytime sky. This seemed to work perfectly. Not only did it illuminate the stealth helicopters, but unbeknownst to Winters at the time, it also fried their rocket targeting systems. Within minutes half of the Felix stealth helicopters were shot down, and the rest had fled because of their targeting systems being offline.

Now the western heavy tanks took on the Felix tanks. There was something to be said for the bravado of these Felix tankers and legionnaires, as they called themselves. They really believed they could stack up against the western Tiger tanks. One hour later, at approximately 6:00 p.m, the entire legion was either dead or falling back into the city.

Because of the losses suffered, Winters again asked for a chance to slow everything down, stressing they had the advantage and needed a chance to regroup. Dietrich denied his request again, stressing the same point back to him, saying, "You have the advantage and need to keep it." Two more continents of armies were en route. If they made it there before that capital fell, the war could be lost.

Winters ordered all heavy tanks into the city with infantry supporting them. The mechanized units to the east of the city were no longer cut off and were able to take out all the remaining artillery entrenchments while the Felix legion was engaged.

They turned the city into a bloodbath. The Easterners used people's homes as sniper hideouts and machine gun nests, using civilians as human shields. They even threw tied-up civilians in front of tanks, knowing our tanks would stop, and then they could be hit with rocket ordinances.

House by house, minute by minute, man by man, the city was cleared. Dietrich sent orders: "Capture or kill Bolton, but do not let him escape." Easier said than done.

CHAPTER 32

DAVID

David was overwhelmed and terrified; he didn't understand why these seemingly demon-like people would care for him and allow him to live. The nurse saw David was awake and came in to speak with him. She told him he would be discharged soon and could go to his new home. David asked who he would be living with, and the nurse laughed, stating whomever he liked, or he could live alone.

None of it was adding up. David assumed it must be an elaborate trick. Nevertheless, he was curious now about what it looked like outside the hospital. He was also grateful that his friends were able to visit him and that they, too, were there. Hopefully, they could all live together.

David got discharged and had a counselor for the division bring him to and show him around his home. David didn't understand. Where was the thought of the environment? Everyone lived together under the experts' decisions to save the planet. His counselor assured him the planet would be fine if they had some privacy.

When David was able to compose himself, he started to realize how nice it would be to have a space of his own. The house was much bigger than the apartment he shared, and now he could set it up however he wanted. He was also ecstatic to learn that he wouldn't have to share his cookware, and they had farms all around he could grab fresh eggs and vegetables from. There were also hunting grounds to hunt for meat, or one could barter.

One of the main differences between living here and in the NWO "colony," as they called it, was the barter system. Rather than paying for things with work credits, people traded valuables; what was not valuable to one might be valuable to someone else. It was an interesting way to live and a great way to live if one had some utility.

The counselor showed David around his home, which was fully furnished. Most of the furniture was simply wood draped in skins of varying dead animals. David didn't like the sight of dead animals, but after feeling the softness of the pelts, he begrudgingly realized how much more comfortable and warm they would be. The counselor told David when the tour was done he should check out the town square. His friends went there every day at noon, and it was 11:30 a.m.

The town square was approximately half a mile from where David lived. He was entranced by all the beautiful foliage he encountered on his walk—tall trees covered in leaves, green grass, bushes. A beautiful array of colors surrounded him, none more beautiful than the mountain peaks that were littered with trees until their halfway points, at which they all became snow covered.

It was colder than David was used to, but the bear pelt he found in his closet kept him warm. David saw his friends at the park, as well as what seemed like thousands of other people, but in reality it was about sixty. David had not seen more than two people in one area outside for some time now.

Katie and Jack were waiting for David. They saw in his face his discomfort at being around so many people, the same discomfort they felt initially. While David was in the hospital, Jack and Katie were able to get used to life here, life the way it was before the world started to change. They walked over to David and assured him everything was fine.

David had all the same questions they had for their counselor when they first went to the town square. What about diseases? What if someone had a weapon? What if someone used language not allowed anymore? They assured him he had nothing to worry about, as they were well protected, pointing to multiple armed guards. For diseases, it was just a risk everyone there was willing to take. When there was a substantial risk of being killed by a bomb every day, a risk from a disease became less significant.

As for language, there was no language not allowed there. There were very few rules. Everyone kept saying they were basically the same as the Ten Commandments from the Old Testament, but the three of them didn't know those. The rules were easy to figure out; basically just do no harm to others physically. Short of that, you were good.

Jack told David he meant to join the military arm of the division. David was beside himself. He was still in shock about everything else, and now his best friend was going to join the military that just destroyed their lives? Jack began to explain to David how he felt the division was what saved their lives. They weren't really living anymore, just merely existing. While death was highly likely fighting against the NWO, it was better than the soft slavery they were under before.

David was relieved to know he'd still have Katie until he learned she planned to join with him. They assured him they didn't begin their training for another three days though, so they would be able to show him around and get him up to speed. "Who knows? Maybe you'll even want to join too by then, David," Katie said.

CHAPTER 33

MICHAEL

Will's minutemen had arrived, the largest of all the rebel groups. Three other groups had come too, with experienced soldiers. The division and its allied rebel groups now comprised a full camp of 1,000,000 and with a rebel military force of roughly 250,000. Michael wished Samson were there to see it.

Will introduced Michael to Colonel Anderson. Michael was shocked to learn of an entire continent of NWO assets being on their side. Colonel Anderson advised Michael of most of the plans of Dietrich. He also advised that Ruiz would likely send his men north, and while they would be outmatched, Colonel Anderson believed they should press their advantage now instead of hunkering down.

Michael had wanted to give his fighters a break for a bit and allow time to train some of the new people they had freed and were wanting to join. But he also knew their only chance at winning the war was with the help of Colonel Anderson's tanks, so he agreed.

Colonel Anderson; Michael; Will; Gomez, the leader of the El Diablo rebels; and McCann, the leader of the Red Beard rebels, all went over a strategy for their fight against Ruiz. Colonel Anderson assured them they would have better success along the coastlines, as the Western European navy would be in the Atlantic with its massive guns, and its aircraft carriers could perform sorties on the advancing southerners.

The problem with hugging the coast was if Ruiz went straight north rather than coming east to fight along the coast, he could wipe out the camp and every stronghold before they could catch up to him. Gomez simply wanted to send everything at Ruiz while the bombers they had left destroyed Ruiz's supply lines. It was not the worst plan, but Ruiz's military was too big and too advanced for that strategy. McCann wanted to hide the bulk of their forces along the most likely path Ruiz was to take and ambush him.

Colonel Anderson wished to hug the coastline and hoped he would be drawn into a fight that would give them every advantage. Meanwhile, Michael and Will wanted to draw everyone back to Canada, move the entire campsite, and use the incoming winter to their advantage. They knew that Ruiz's arrogance and his men's lack of gear for the cold would lead to disaster.

Finally, a plan was agreed upon, a slight hybrid. The force would be split in half, with one half going to the coastline in the hopes of drawing Ruiz that way, and the other half would set up multiple defensive lines in case Ruiz went straight north. The defensive lines would begin approximately three hundred miles north of the South American and North American border. Every step of those three hundred miles would be laden with ambushing soldiers, mines, and traps.

On the coast would be Colonel Anderson and the bulk of the mechanized units, partly because it was his plan to be there but largely because they would be able to catch up quickly in case Ruiz did head straight north. If Ruiz did decide to go straight north, Anderson would be able to cut off their supply lines, and then they could strike Ruiz from the south and the east.

The leaders had their orders; now they went to tell their men.

CHAPTER 34

BOLTON

Bolton was being given updates minute by minute, hour by hour. His generals worried with every mile taken by Winters's army, but Bolton's plan wasn't to fight for the dirt or to protect the citizens. He wanted to draw them into the capital, where he would unleash every gun at his disposal and the Felix Legion nearby. He hoped that the other NWO contingents would have arrived by then, but he was not worried if they had not.

Bolton didn't go to a bunker like his generals and aides had suggested. He instead chose to move his command center to a mountaintop just outside the city so he could watch as the battle began. He wanted to have complete control over every move made. This worried the generals; while they all respected Bolton's military knowledge, too much micromanagement was never a good thing.

"Finally!" Bolton exclaimed as he saw the first mechanized units of the western army closing. His artillery commanders asked permission to fire on them. Bolton denied this request. He said to pull them all in closer. He wanted them to believe the city would fall easily, and then the ground would shake with their heavy guns.

The western lighter tanks began to split and surround the city. Now Bolton gave the order, and all hell broke loose. Even from their position on the mountaintop, they could feel the vibrations from the massive artillery guns and explosions. Without waiting to see how well the strikes had done, Bolton ordered the Felix legion to engage.

Bolton knew their tank technology would have been thwarted, as Dietrich was a part of the team that created it. But no one from the West knew of their helicopter technology. While Bolton's generals seemed uneasy about the way things were going, Bolton was seemingly as confident as ever. His faith in the Felix legion was supreme.

The mood on the mountaintop changed as they all witnessed the helicopters deliver blow after blow on the mechanized units. The Felix Legion requested permission to circle around the city, taking out all the smaller mechanized units and freeing up the artillery to begin barraging the main force again.

Bolton refused. He wanted the entire army crushed, and crushed now. "Press the attack to their center and split their line," he ordered. The Felix legion, not known for listening to orders they didn't like, chose to follow this one. Maybe for fear if they didn't, they would seem cowardly for choosing the weaker opponent. Or maybe they truly thought it was the right move, but it was disastrous.

The sky was illuminated with thousands of flares, blinding for everyone on the field and on the mountaintop overlooking the battle. Then the invisible helicopters started being shot down. Bolton was beside himself. "Flares? Flares are what defeats this technology?" he said. He ordered one of his aides to send word that whoever didn't account for that was to be executed for treason along with their family.

Now Bolton did not seem so confident on this hill. He saw his artillery encampments had all been overrun. He should have let the Felix legion free them. Now the worst and most unexpected calamity: the western army was driving back the Felix legion. The Felix legion had never lost a battle—until now.

Bolton ordered all remaining men inside the city to stay and fight till the end. Anyone caught retreating would be killed as a traitor. He then ordered the Felix Legion to regroup on the mountaintop to escort him east.

While all the chaos was erupting, Bolton received some ill-timed good news. The other continents had arrived; however, they were six hundred miles east, and it would take them two days to get here. Bolton knew the city was lost and ordered a retreat to the east.

CHAPTER 35

WINTERS

Winters sent word to Dietrich. They had taken the capital, but there was no sign of Bolton. The Felix legion had turned course while they were routing and began to head straight east. They could be transporting him.

Dietrich replied, "Use the communications system in the capital to let everyone under NWO occupation around the world know that there is hope, and then send units to hunt down and kill Bolton." Winters knew it was a suicide mission, but he also knew it was vital to the effort, and the cause he was fighting for was bigger than the lives it would cost to kill Bolton.

To catch up to the Felix Legion, it would have to be the faster smaller mechanized units. Winters also knew since the force would be split, a defense of the capital wouldn't be viable, so he requested from Dietrich to allow the heavy mechanized units and anyone not needed for this mission to retreat back behind western defensive positions. Dietrich allowed this request.

Winters gathered the commanders of his first armored division. As it was the first one the West had, it was mostly composed of older but smaller and faster mechanized units. He told them the task set out before them and offered for any man who wished to be sent West and not partake. Winters knew his men, though, and the only question they had was who had been picked to lead this mission. Winters replied it was him, and all the tank commanders nodded in acknowledgment. He was a senior commander, so he could order someone else to do this. He had children, as did many of the soldiers, but he had a way home to them, and he was choosing this mission. Winters knew his men and the ferocity they would fight with if he was with them, which would be needed to take on the Felix legion at such a limited strength of their own.

Winters radioed to Dietrich that the plan was in place, and he would personally radio Dietrich when the mission was complete. Dietrich didn't expect Winters to go himself. They had served together their entire career, so he didn't want it, but he knew better than to try to stop Winters. Dietrich replied, "Godspeed, and I will see you again, my friend."

CHAPTER 36

DIETRICH

Dietrich never wanted a leadership position in the military; he always wanted to remain a man on the ground. This was what made him a better leader than most and someone his men would do anything for.

Unlike Bolton's wife, Nancy, Dietrich's wife, Angela, was proud of how her husband acted in these moments. She never cared for the status or anything that came with his position; she loved the man, and these moments reminded her why. For him to care so deeply about everyone under his command reaffirmed her knowledge of how good of a man she married was.

Angela awoke at 5:00 a.m. to find Dietrich sitting on their balcony staring out into the predawn sky. She sat next to him but didn't say a word. She knew in these moments, there was nothing she could say that would help. While Dietrich wouldn't admit it, he enjoyed her being there with him. The moment didn't last long. A knock came at the door; it startled Angela, but Dietrich was unfazed. He knew it meant contact had been made, and it had begun. Dietrich leaned over, kissed Angela, and told her he would be back as soon as possible.

Dietrich was driven to the command center and told that Colonel Anderson and the air force had engaged NWO forces chasing down survivors. They had won the first skirmish. This news seemed to be joyous to his aide, but to Dietrich, it was not. He knew even with victory came death for his men.

Once at the command post, Dietrich gave the order for Winters to proceed and strike east. Anderson's report was one of very good news; the rebel forces were much larger and better equipped than expected.

They still were not capable of a one-on-one with an NWO force, but they were nothing to be scoffed at.

However, this good news was accompanied by bad news. Admiral Copeland, looking furious, entered the command post and stated that they had lost 3 carriers (they had 17 more), 35 destroyers (they had 377 more), and 12 supply ships. It seemed Ruiz had sent his submarines north in anticipation of this betrayal. Dietrich ordered half of his carriers to be sent to the East Coast, escorted by half of the destroyers, with constant sonar flyovers of the seas. The other half of his carriers, along with the remaining destroyers and the rest of his fleet, were directed into the channel.

While not expecting a naval battle because of their naval superiority, Dietrich still prepared for one. Even though he could certainly send his navy in search of these subs and eliminate them that way, that would come at a heavy price, much heavier than this plan that had been devised.

The other generals in the room were astonished that Copeland liked this plan. Copeland had a reputation of an intense fighter, who liked to press his enemies. He liked this plan because he devised the trap years ago. Copeland was the admiral for the UK navy, and in secret they had laid massive webs of submarine traps all along the English Channel knowing how much submarines devastated them in WWI and WWII. Since it was a secret plan and Copeland did not trust the new NWO leadership, no one knew of it, until recently, when he told Dietrich. The plan relied on them being chased into the channel.

The navy's orders were dispatched. Dietrich had his coffee in hand and told his aide to leave the pot as he would be drinking it constantly. Dietrich gave up alcohol once the NWO took over, the only good thing in his life to come from it. But since then he was never caught without a coffee.

Word of Winters's success reached Dietrich constantly. Dietrich knew no amount of land gained would be worth anything if Bolton was able to escape. Dietrich ordered an eastern wall be constructed with all haste. Massive defensive entrenchments with heavy guns were to be placed every one hundred meters, with crisscrossing fields of concertina wire laden with minefields in between them, in case Winters needed to fall back.

Dietrich was told of the Felix Legion's engagement. He was enraged; he couldn't believe Bolton would use mercenaries when he called himself such a great military mind. Dietrich was beside himself when he was informed of the cloaked helicopters. He knew how devastating attack helicopters were to tanks in general, especially with them now being cloaked. He couldn't imagine the psychological effect that was having on his men.

Dietrich ordered their top engineers to begin working on a system to break through the camouflage. Word was sent to Winters to attempt to capture a downed helicopter if possible so it could be reverse engineered.

Word came that the city had been captured, but not Bolton. Dietrich sent an order to Winters to hunt him down and this time not to try to capture him but to just kill.

CHAPTER 37

RUIZ

Ruiz was furious. He expected the betrayal, but he did not foresee them having fighter aircraft in North America so quickly. Ruiz ordered a full advance north. He knew that Colonel Anderson and three mechanized western brigades had arrived to assist the rebels, but it wouldn't be enough. Ruiz's mechanized units outnumbered those three brigades two to one, and he also had attack helicopters with some strong infantry units.

Ruiz's men made it to the border, and their intel reported that the forces had split. Colonel Anderson and the bulk of his mechanized units were on the coast, covered by their navy. Straight north of them were ragtag rebels with a few western tank groups meshed in.

Ruiz's generals wanted to strike Anderson head-on, stating if they took him out, then the rebels stood no chance. But Ruiz's generals didn't know the effect multiple carriers could have even on an advanced force with AA. Ruiz knew if he struck north, Anderson would then try to trap him and cut off his supply lines.

Ruiz decided they would strike north with all haste, taking only with them essential supplies, such as oil and food. The rest of the supply line they would sever themselves. Ruiz was banking on quickly crushing the forces to his north and making it to the rebel encampment to destroy it. Even if Anderson was behind his men, they would have fortified positions and could resupply via air or from their navy on the Pacific.

Ruiz's tanks were moving with all haste and steamrolling all the resistance they met. Thus far it had been nothing but sporadic mines, which usually only damaged the tank temporarily, or poor shots from handheld antitank rocket devices. This plan seemed to be working flawlessly despite his generals' misgivings about it.

The forward tanks began taking sustained casualties. They had made it as far north as a few miles outside the Abrams Mountain. Maybe it was arrogance or just a feeling of haste, but they didn't even see the encamped western tanks in old camouflage on the hilltops aside the pathway. They now knew they were close to an encampment.

Ruiz's tanks got pinned down, and dozens got shredded by the tanks and now artillery guns from inside the mountain. The explosions were biblical, and flesh and metal went flying with every blast. If you were lucky enough to survive the blast, the heat was felt for hours like a stinging that didn't leave. Ruiz's tank commander ordered a fallback, which was quickly overturned by Ruiz himself. He wanted the tanks to stay put and engage as best they could.

Every minute that passed, more of Ruiz's tanks were getting shredded, but he knew his Apaches were en route, and if they fell back, the western tanks would hide in the mountainside. After losing thirty-two of their best tanks, the Apaches finally arrived.

The Apaches did their work quickly, with rocket barrage after rocket barrage destroying the tanks on the hilltop. Some AA batteries fired back, but the Apache pilots were able to flare out and evade them with ease. Now the attack pressed forward into the mountain.

CHAPTER 38

DAVID

David had joined Katie and Jack at the park today as it was their last day before they "ship out." The day was beautiful, colder than David was used to still, but he was beginning to like the way the crisp air felt and how the bear or, today, wolf skin pelt, felt on him.

Jack asked David if he had given any more thought on joining them in the military arm of the division. David replied, "Absolutely not." While he was beginning to understand why Jack and Katie wanted to, he never would. David said if he ever began to believe he was truly lied to the entire time, then he would find another way to serve the division, but it wouldn't be killing those he once saw as his heroes.

Katie put a stop to that conversation, saying they should all spend the last day they would have in a while talking about something more pleasant. She asked David how he had been adjusting and how he had been doing with food now that it was not simply delivered to his door. David replied he had been eating just the eggs and vegetables in his neighborhood farmed for everyone, but he had grown an interest in attempting to hunt for meat.

This was a shock to Katie and Jack but a welcomed one. They told him how the best meal they had ever had was when they hunted the animal themselves and then praised God for the animal and prayed over its soul. David was dumbfounded at how quickly they had taken to this new lifestyle, and Jack and Katie could see it in his face. They told him he would get there too. They found it very strange, the praying and belief in someone in the clouds, but now they couldn't deny his presence. They felt him everywhere.

Then a strange noise was heard. It was not the same as an air raid alarm, so neither Jack nor Katie knew what this one meant. Then they saw men from the military arm of the division running past them, weapons in hand, and yelling for all civilians to head to the bunkers. David was terrified again, a feeling he hated but continued to feel. Jack and Katie told him to go. He asked them if they were coming, and they said no, as they were done running. David stood there frozen as Jack and Katie yelled at him to go to the bunker, then both turned and ran alongside the soldiers.

Before they could get far, a loud explosion was heard. The outer fortifications of the town had been destroyed. The passageway throughout the mountains was too tight and laden with traps for tanks, but a massive wave of NWO infantry came pouring through. David hadn't moved. He was just in the middle of the park, stuck in fear like quicksand pulling him deeper and deeper. The more he wanted to move, the less he could. Division soldiers were behind him, next to him, and in front of him. They were all being mercilessly cut down by the NWO soldiers.

David watched in horror, and then he saw his friend Jack shot in the chest and drop to the ground. Katie dove on his body almost instinctively to cover him. An NWO soldier walked up to them and put his gun to the back of Katie's head and executed her while she was trying to protect Jack. David heard an almost shrieking scream from a wounded Jack beneath Katie's now lifeless body. David saw the soldier chuckle, level his silver handgun at Jack's face, and squeeze the trigger again. They didn't have weapons; they had no means of fighting. Katie was just lying on Jack's body. The veil was falling off; David was seeing his "heroes" for who they truly were. He would never forget this "hero's" face.

David started to feel something he had never felt before. The quicksand was leaving, and the fear was being replaced with an unquenchable rage. Without thinking he picked up a rifle from a fallen division soldier next to him and began firing. David had never fired a weapon before, but now he was firing one with lethal precision. Almost every trigger pulled led to an NWO soldier dropping. It did not matter; his rage was unrelenting. David began hearing someone saying, "Move, shoot, move!"

Listening to whoever or whatever this was, he was now shooting, then moving to a new position, then shooting, then moving to a new position. David, still dressed as a civilian in the division, gave a morale boost to all the soldiers. The fighting intensified. But there were too many NWO soldiers. Some of the division soldiers were beginning to retreat, but David wasn't a soldier, and he was not driven by the battle; he was driven by rage.

David kept fighting, and then miraculously, men dressed in US/UK/French/German military uniforms arrived from behind David, hundreds, if not thousands, of them. They won the day.

It took them a minute to get the rifle from David's hands. David didn't respond to anyone and just had a blank stare, similar to the one he had in Lexington, but very different. He was brought to medical to be checked out, and hours later he came to, without remembering much but knowing he was now a changed man. David joined the military arm the next day, and the men who witnessed his actions in the battle were happy to have him among their ranks.

CHAPTER 39

MICHAEL

Michael and Will were both in the bunker monitoring the situation. It seemed as though ill news came constantly. McCann's ambushes and mines were hardly having an effect. They hadn't expected Ruiz's force to be so close so soon.

Hour by hour they were getting closer and closer. Michael had decided not to order an evacuation of the encampment north to Canada, citing all the infrastructure they had built here was too valuable to give up. Many of his generals, especially Dondarion, did not like this decision. The mountains were perfect for ambushes. He could have gotten every civilian north to Canada and set tanks on every hilltop.

But Michael's order was respected. As the South American's military drove nearer and nearer, uneasiness set in. When the outer perimeter defenses were reached, the alarms were sounded for all civilians to head down to the bunkers. Michael, Will, Spear, Gomez, and Dondarion all went up in the opposite direction. They did not mean to hide out in the bunker while their infantry fought on the ground.

When they reached the surface, they could hear the gunfire approaching closer and saw roughly two hundred division men dug in along a freshy built trench line. The generals split up and joined the men. To their surprise the shooting wasn't approaching. It was intense and rapid, but it seemed as though whatever division soldiers were ahead were holding them off. Michael, Will, and Dondarion took one hundred men with them and moved forward to join the fight, leaving Spear back to hold the fallback line.

They were moving as rapidly as they could to assist their men in the front. When they got close, they saw not only division soldiers but also civilians—civilians who defied the alarm bells to go for safety and instead took up arms to fight for their new home. Men, women, even some young and some old. This sight surely gave the men with the generals an immense jolt as they joined the fight.

This battle raged on for what felt like days but in reality was hours. The civilians, while courageous, were not faring well, and the division medics were getting torn down whenever they would leave their cover to try to save them. They were losing this fight. Michael was about to order a fallback to the trench line when he heard a loud noise that sounded like a horn, and then he could hear Spear and others screaming war cries behind him. He turned and saw Spear sprinting forward with what must have been thousands of Anderson's infantry.

The division took many casualties, mostly civilian, but they won the day and held the entry point. Michael also learned something about Anderson. He might say he was doing one thing, but he made plans of his own. Most would be angered by his seeming deceitfulness, but his deceit and switching of the plans without anyone's knowledge surely saved them. Michael just hoped Anderson had enough men to overtake the South American rear guard.

CHAPTER 40

WINTERS

Winters and about thirty thousand of his men were chasing down the fleeing Felix units. It had been twenty-eight hours that they had been chasing, and to their surprise there had been limited rearguard attacks from the fleeing men. Winters believed this was leading them to a trap, but he knew it was suicide anyway, and to slow their pace would lessen their chances of killing Bolton.

Finally, the trail seemed to stop, just inside a sprawling city. Winters ordered a few fast-moving lightly armored vehicles ahead to scout which direction the enemy fled outside the city, but it appeared they hadn't fled. Then the city erupted.

Artillery was coming in unlike anything these soldiers had faced. Winters began ordering a defensive perimeter to be set up and for the soldiers to get inside any structure and fortify it. He knew what this meant. It would be urban warfare, block by block, house by house.

The shelling was followed by bombers leveling entire buildings, and exchanges of small arms fire as NWO troops and Felix legion troops attempted to gain entry into some of the buildings on the defensive perimeter. Almost all the tanks were destroyed by the artillery and bombings. Winters couldn't get an accurate count, but he believed he had likely lost half his force.

The shelling stopped. Winters expected a massive ground assault, but it didn't come, so he quickly took count of the men he had left and the casualties sustained. Of the thirty thousand he chased after the legion with, seventeen thousand were alive, but only twelve thousand were in fighting shape. Winters sucked in the defensive perimeter, asking for volunteers to remain at the outer perimeter hidden, and to enact strikes from behind the encroaching enemy. Every one of those volunteers knew their death was imminent, but so was the death of everyone who remained; however, their death could buy more time to accomplish the mission.

Two more days went by without any real attempts to push into their perimeter. Now Winters saw why; their western and southern flanks were surrounded by men from the other NWO continents. They knew these men were coming, but they didn't expect them to be here this soon. He knew they would not be able to accomplish the mission of killing Bolton.

Winters had requested the NWO care for their wounded, a request he made simply to buy time, but to his surprise it was a request they honored. The wounded were transported outside the defensive perimeter, and the NWO medics took them to hospitals nearby and displayed it all on film in the city center so they knew it was really happening and not a trick.

The NWO then began blasting over the public adress systems a message on repeat, saying that any soldier who surrendered would not only be forgiven but would also be able to choose to have their purpose back in the military of the NWO. They offered full rank and pay to anyone who surrendered. Winters gathered his captains together and ordered them to tell all the men that if any of them wished to surrender, they could. He would not be surrendering, but he would not begrudge any man his own choice.

The following morning Winters's captains reported to him that of the thirteen thousand in fighting condition, six thousand wished to surrender, and seven thousand chose to follow him to a certain death. Winters told the captains to tell the men they fought bravely, and he would see them again in the next life. A total of six thousand men then walked outside the perimeter and were taken into custody by the NWO.

Winters expected an all-out assault, figuring they'd know he only had less than one-third of his force left, but it didn't come that night. The next morning they awoke to the sounds of helicopters and flares. They looked outside to see Chinook transport helicopters carrying large nets. Some of the men thought it was another goodwill gesture, and they were sending food supplies. Then the nets dropped.

The heads of all six thousand men who surrendered the night before were dropped to the ground in the city center. The flares going off were atop the tallest buildings, where the bodies of the six thousand men without heads were hung upside down. Now the video screens showed the wounded who had surrendered being tortured, mutilated, and cut a part piece by piece in the hospital. This was the NWO they all knew; this was why Winters and the other seven thousand men were not going to surrender. They knew their fate, and they were not going to meet it voluntarily.

Winters made a last order to his men who were surrounded by machine gun nests, snipers, mortars, minefields, and so on: "Fix bayonets." His captains thought he was losing his mind, but he repeated the order, and they listened. He asked one captain, Leopold, to embark on a different mission: find a way to send a message to Dietrich and tell him the hell their men experienced there.

Leopold tried to refuse the order and wished to stay and die alongside his brothers and leader. Winters explained to him that his mission was more important; the rest of the military needed to know what awaited them if they surrendered. They all knew they would be brutal, but this was a new level of brutality. The truth of what happened here needed to escape and not be buried by those tyrants. Leopold asked if someone else could be chosen, and Winters told him that question was why it must be him.

Winters told Leopold to leave at the sound of the charge. Winters led his six thousand men screaming and charging toward the enemy positions. To his captains' dismay, many of the NWO were caught off guard or simply ran away. They were not only recapturing their outer perimeter, but they were also advancing blocks away from their original perimeter. It seemed like a brutal massacre of all who stood in their way. All the men were screaming like the Viking or native warriors of history, and all were taking many lives in vengeance.

Winters's bayonet charge with his six thousand men killed three times their number in enemy combatants. But eventually, they all fell.

CHAPTER 41

DIETRICH

Word reached Dietrich that Winters and his men were massacred. Bolton's men had stripped their bodies and cut them to pieces and displayed them through the emergency broadcast system for all the world to see. It came on the screen in the headquarters, and Dietrich saw them cutting up Winters's body.

He gave no reaction, but everyone in the room knew they were close, and this was unpleasant for all to see. Bolton thought this would put fear in his adversaries, a mistake many tyrants had made before.

Dietrich very calmly ordered the island of England's infantry to be sent to the eastern wall that was created and for all AA assets to be sent there. He knew Bolton would throw everything at this wall, and if he didn't, the navy would be able to thwart any attempt at a land invasion on the islands of England or Ireland.

Dietrich sent word to Colonel Anderson, informing him of the situation and telling him to treat any NWO captured as they treated General Winters. His aide then drove him back to his quarters. Angela was waiting for him.

The emergency broadcasts went out over every TV, and Angela knew Winters's face well. While she had never seen the horrors of war like this before, she knew how close her husband was to him and knew he needed her now.

Dietrich gave Angela a hug and a kiss and went to the balcony to sit outside. She gave him a moment then followed. When she sat next to him, he asked, "Did I do the right thing?" She was beside herself; she was not expecting this question, nor was she ever expecting her husband to ever have doubts when he had always been so sure of himself.

She told him, "It does not matter what I think. I had a good life before this war, and I still have a good life. What matters is what all the people who would have been dead in America and other places right now think. I know your closest friend was just killed brutally. I saw it too. But that was a price you all knew and you all accepted individually. Unless you believe your friend's life is worth a lifetime of slavery and death for millions of others, or you believe for a second he at any point, knowing the consequences, would have made a different decision, I don't know why you're asking me this question."

Dietrich's sorrow and grief were replaced with an almost shameful feeling. Angela was right; it was okay to mourn the loss of a friend, but to think one life, any life, was worth more than the millions in servitude when you both knew the costs but signed the dotted line to pay it anyway was a moment of weakness, one that he subconsciously knew to only have in his own home with the woman he loved and not in front of the men.

Dietrich spent a few hours with Angela, thanked her, then called his aide to take him back to the headquarters. Before he left, Angela told him she had never been prouder, and while it wouldn't matter because they would win this war, she was happy to die for the right cause. Dietrich had a reaffirmed resolve, and he responded, "We will both live for the right cause."

CHAPTER 42

ANDERSON

Anderson and his men set out. He requested a dozen recon drones from the carrier group based off the East Coast to spot Ruiz and let him know immediately of the force's intentions. He also didn't make great haste in his move to the coast. He knew he didn't need to. If Ruiz was to fall for the bait trap to the coast, it mattered not if they met south or north of the Mason–Dixon line from the civil war; the naval airpower would decimate them regardless.

Anderson received intel from the naval assets that Ruiz was pushing straight forward to the camp, which was precisely why he chose such a slow approach to the coast. Anderson anticipated this move, so now he sent his infantry straight back to the camp to defend it. All infantry fighting vehicles and all vehicles aside from main battle tanks capable of carrying personnel were to be utilized to expedite this movement of troops.

The rest of the mechanized units and the colonel himself would lead an assault far south of the line and cut off any chance of resupply or reinforcement to Ruiz. Anderson sent word to Dietrich that the entire South American land forces could be wiped out in this mission, but he would need support from the navy's aircraft. Anderson was given permission to use them on any sortie close to the coastline, but Ruiz's position would force these aircraft to travel for hours before reaching their targets, thus leaving the carrier groups themselves vulnerable.

Anderson knew this but made the urgent plea anyway. If the South American land forces could be eliminated, they could free South America and have a united continent and the Western Europe to fight from. They could help to even the odds. Anderson did not know how Dietrich would respond to this request, but it mattered not; he pressed on with his plan.

As his mechanized units reached the rear guard and supply lines of the South American force, they tore through them like a hot knife through butter. Most of the South American forces fled at the sight of these tanks. They were the same types and models that their military had, but the symbols on them that many had painted themselves helped instill fear in the enemy.

Anderson's troops knew what was said about the rebels and what was said about them. They chose to use that to their advantage. The tanks, while being painted in national camouflage patterns, had symbols and illustrations affixed to them that were normal for wars seen in the past but now were of a time long gone and achieved likely a greater instilling of fear in the enemy than ever before in history.

Quickly the most fearsome symbol to be seen by adversaries of this newly formed military force was a large man seated with a massive spear. Many tanks had this symbol on their underbelly and two on either side of their turret. Unbeknownst to the South American NWO soldiers, this symbol represented the old Norse Viking god Odin, and the tanks that bore it were only one regiment of mechanized units from all of Anderson's force. But their reputation made them seem larger than an entire division.

Anderson's plan was to wait, dig in, and thwart any attempt at freeing the South American forces trapped north of him. He wanted to let the naval airpower destroy them while he mopped up any who retreated.

CHAPTER 43

RUIZ

Ruiz saw the entrance was too narrow for tanks to have any sort of effective mobility, and they would be very vulnerable. He ordered an infantry division through while the mechanized units would hold the entrance. His scouts had already reported to him that Anderson had cut off his southern flank; it mattered not. Now Ruiz knew there were no experienced soldiers in front of him, just rebels waiting to be slaughtered like the lambs they were.

Reports and updates were coming to the Command Post by the minute of the success of the infantry. They had established control of the entry point and were pushing forward, killing all in their wake. Ruiz was always one to insist on the need of keeping laborers, but not these folk; rebellion was a virus that must be eradicated by fire.

Ruiz's tank commanders requested to head south and engage Anderson, but Ruiz refused, saying, "Let Anderson come to us, or let him sit there behind us while this camp they sent so many resources to defend is exterminated. Then when his mission has failed, we will take him and his men out." Ruiz grew bored in the CP; he was not usually one to join the combat, but he didn't believe this was real combat, just slaughter.

Ruiz and his security detail made their way to the front, where his infantry was advancing steadily. They waded through a wake of hundreds of bodies. Men, women, children, some armed, some with no weapons near them. This was welcome news to Ruiz's eyes. He was not a particularly brutal man, but he was a practical one. He didn't relish in the death of unarmed combatants, but he also didn't want any rebel to have the ability to kill his men later. It was a love for his soldiers rather than a hatred for those he was fighting that caused his brutality. While an unarmed woman or child might be no threat in this instance, they could flee and spread their rebel virus. Or take up arms later. That was why it was to be a brutal campaign.

That was also why he was relieved to see his men following his orders. Ruiz's men were not like the Felix legion or the NWO assigned to Yelden in North America. He saw it pained them to do this, but whether they agreed with Ruiz's reasoning, they followed their orders anyway.

The fighting was barely fighting. The shots from the civilians were as accurate as a blind man's would be. Ruiz even joked with his security detachment that they would suffer more casualties fighting a blind army. They were systematically advancing but were slowed constantly not by enemy fire but by the awe of what they were surrounded by—wooden homes, gardens, parks, things most of them hadn't seen in a long time and some had never before witnessed. It almost felt wrong destroying a people who lived like this and were able to construct all this while living on the run. Ruiz thought of how useful they could have been, but it didn't matter; they chose their lot.

The attack pressed forward. Ruiz saw a civilian shot in the chest by one of his men. "Excellent shot," Ruiz thought. "Perfectly center mass likely in the heart from the blood spurting out. He'll be one less combatant to worry about soon." Ruiz saw a woman dove on top of this man crying and attempting to shield him from further gunfire. Ruiz walked up to them, slung his rifle, and took out his silver-plated .44 magnum revolver. He placed it at the back of the sobbing woman's head and squeezed the trigger. The man beneath her was horrified. He was now covered in this woman's brain matter as her head exploded like a watermelon from the power of the .44 magnum. Ruiz heard the man let out a bloodcurdling scream as he painfully took his last breath. Then Ruiz pointed the muzzle of his revolver at the man's face and squeezed the trigger.

Even Ruiz wasn't prepared for what a .44 magnum would do at that close range. Both heads were cut to pieces almost as if squished by the hands of a giant. Blood and guts were splattered everywhere. Ruiz didn't do this act because he wanted to; he did it to show his men they wouldn't be the only ones getting their hands dirty. Ruiz was a religious man himself; he did what he did to try to help his men follow their orders, but he knew he had just condemned his soul to eternity in hell.

Suddenly, the fighting became more fierce. It was still just rebels, but the savage acts not only performed by Ruiz but also by others under his command had seemed to breathe new life and morale into the rebels. This was also a desired effect for Ruiz; if they ran and hid, they could ambush his men, which would be much deadlier than his seasoned, trained soldiers engaging these ragtag rebels in open combat.

Ruiz and his men began to get to semi covered positions as some of the rebels were now finding their shots. Casualties were to be expected in a battle, and it was going to happen eventually. One hundred more rebels had joined the fight, but it didn't matter, as it meant there were more lambs to be slaughtered.

Then Ruiz heard a loud blasting noise. He couldn't make out what it was at first, but when he realized what it was, he was confused. It was a horn; horns hadn't been used in war in a long time. He heard it again but couldn't tell from where; he didn't see anyone holding a horn. But then he heard screaming and saw thousands running toward him and his men's position. These were not rebels. His intel was wrong.

Ruiz's security told him it was time to leave, but he didn't want to order a retreat. He was not about to tell Bolton he lost a battle to rebels. And then it all went black.

CHAPTER 44

MARY

Mary was loving this life she was living with Jeff. She didn't like that he now wore a military uniform, only because she was afraid he would have to fight in actual combat. But he assured her he was in an intelligence unit, and his unit would always be far from the front. He tried telling her about history and how in all wars, but none more so than WWII, the intelligence units were vital in winning the war.

Mary was trying to grow an interest in history as she realized she was living it and could certainly learn from others who had lived in similar circumstances. But it was still foreign to her. When she was young, she had no interest in history, and when she was an adult, the teaching of most history was outlawed by the NWO.

Mary also just wanted to spend every moment she had with Jeff, focusing on the positives and soaking up every moment they got to spend outside in the park or at one of the theater halls built or inside their own home together, trying to have children the old way. She knew this new life and new world could be taken from them at any moment, so while she understood the importance of learning, now more than ever, she would rather learn on her own time or from others when Jeff was with the military rather than waste a second they were together.

Mary and Jeff had also found a few other couples whom they hang out with. One couple, Conor and Morgan, had been with the division since its inception. Mary usually asked them to teach her about history since the division made that a cornerstone for all their citizens to learn upon. Then there were Dan and Lindsay. Lindsay had been with the division from the beginning, but Dan, like Mary, didn't know they even existed until they liberated their city. Then there were Andrae and Raleigh. Mary had the most in common with them because they were also set up by the NWO. Andrae had secretly been helping the rebels, as had Jeff, without Raleigh's knowledge. But like Mary, Raleigh chose to stay with him and follow him and chose love over the state, and neither of them could be happier with the decision they made.

They were all hanging out, having dinner and a few drinks. Dan was dancing as he always did. Andrae and Jeff were pretending not to talk about the war but very plainly were talking about it just in whispers. Mary, the rest of the ladies, and Conor were all playing drinking games and cheering on Dan dancing. Then they heard an alarm. Mary was the newest member to the division, but even she knew what this alarm meant. Thankfully, since Jeff worked for the division, their home was close to the entranceway to the bunker, so they all began making their way there. Conor took a little longer, only to catch up later holding all the beers, saying, "If we're going to be in a bunker, might as well keep the party going."

As they approached the bunker, Jeff and Andrae got really silent. They were all moving very fast, so Mary assumed it was just because they were out of breath. Then they made it to the bunker. Jeff recognized the guards at the entrance and went over and spoke with them. Mary, Andrae, and Raleigh waited for him to return. Only he didn't. As the guard began walking over, Andrae began telling Raleigh that he and Jeff had to go to protect them all. They were just intelligence, but they couldn't sit in the bunker when the fight was brought to their homes. Raleigh began to cry. Mary didn't believe him though. Jeff would not go to fight without saying goodbye.

The guard reached Mary, saying, "Jeff told me to tell you he knows you would have latched on to him and not let him leave, so he couldn't say goodbye in person, but he will be back. And if he doesn't come back, here is this." The guard handed her a letter. Now Mary was crying too. Dan and Conor both looked back; they now saw what was happening. They looked at each other, chugged a beer each, and then said goodbye to their wives and followed Andrae and Jeff. Mary tried to go with them, but Jeff told the guard she was pregnant. The division welcomed females joining the fight but did not allow pregnant women to serve in any capacity. Childbirth was seen as the highest service to the division.

Because of Jeff and Andrae's status, none of the wives were allowed to leave the bunker. Jeff and Andrae knew what they were about to witness. They had read the reports and seen glimpses of it before. They hoped Conor and Dan would stay in the bunker too, but they wouldn't stop them if they tried to come. The women, though, they knew they couldn't live with themselves if the women only joined the fighting because of them. So they ordered the guards to hold them inside the bunker, and the guards did. They did not envy the guards because they knew how fierce their wives could be, but they had to focus.

Focus was all Mary could do now—focus on her world being destroyed. The other women began to pray. Mary had prayed a few times with Jeff, but it never felt right. Now it was all she could do. While it didn't relieve all the fear, it certainly helped. Mary prayed and prayed, not just for Jeff but also for all their friends and for everyone taking up arms in defense of everyone inside the bunker and all the bunkers throughout the division's camp.

Mary was never a political person, never someone who cared who was president or leader or even really knew the difference. But now that she saw people who just wanted to be left alone to live their own lives were being attacked, she couldn't help but feel a rage and a desire to help change that, in whatever capacity she could. Either help to make it so the attacks stopped or help to make it so the attackers were crushed and could never attack again. Suddenly, Mary felt very ill and began vomiting. The prayers stopped as all the women moved to care for her.

Mary woke up in a hospital bed. Everything seemed normal, with no sounds of gunfire, and she was not in a bunker. She saw the division's symbols everywhere, so she breathed a sigh of relief. She asked the nurse what happened and if they were safe. The nurse told her that they were, the NWO scum were beaten, and that she had visitors waiting for her to wake up. Mary began to cry tears of joy. They won, and she would be reunited with Jeff in a moment.

She saw a group of people walking in—Dan, Conor, Raleigh, Morgan, Lindsay, Andrae, and Michael, the leader of the division. She asked if Jeff was hurt and when she could see him. Her questions were met with silence; no one wanted to answer. Michael then cleared his throat and said, "I'm sorry, but Jeff didn't make it." Mary went from crying tears of joy to sobbing and wailing. The entire hospital could hear the pain in her cries. The ladies all rushed to her and cried with her. The men, as men often do in these situations, stood there unsure of exactly what to do or what to say.

Michael continued with "I want you to know he died a hero. He did not have to be there, and if I had known he was there, him and Andrae, I would have dragged them away myself. Their mission of intelligence is more important than the fighting. But that's not who he is, which is why you loved him, why I loved him, why we all loved him. He died shielding civilians running to the bunkers. His act saved lives. I know this will not wash away the pain, but know that without him, more would have died. When I reached him, he was still alive. His dying words were to tell you he is sorry and that now he can protect you always from above."

Mary just continued to cry. She asked to be alone, but none of her friends moved; they knew she didn't actually want to be alone. Michael did leave but not before kissing her forehead, touching her belly, and saying, "I hope you name him Jeff and he one day grows up to be like his father." Mary's tears continued, but the sobs stopped; she is confused. She was not pregnant. They had been trying, but it hadn't worked. Then her friends all looked at her and tried to smile through the tears. Morgan was the first of her friends to speak and said, "Your child will have a bigger family than any of us had." Somehow in all the pain, they all laughed at that. Mary asked them if it was true, and they called the nurse over, who confirmed she was pregnant.

Mary was beside herself; she didn't want to raise a child without Jeff. But she didn't have a choice, and she felt strengthened and grateful for her friends. She didn't know what compelled her to, but she looked up at the ceiling as if looking up to God or Jeff and smiled. It started to make sense to her, as if it was being whispered through a flashback. She was throwing up in the tunnel because she was pregnant. She started to feel this rage and will to fight, which was very against her nature but was very much so in Jeff's nature. Her emotions and being had already begun to change because of the life forming inside her that was part her and part Jeff. Then she remembered she was given a letter to read if Jeff didn't come back.

She tried again asking them all to leave, but she knew they wouldn't. When they saw her take out the letter though, they did leave the hospital room to give her some privacy. She struggled to open the letter with the tears blanketing the paper and her hands shaking. She finally got it open, and in typical Jeff fashion, it was a long handwritten letter. She chuckled at the first sight of his awful script handwriting, which he constantly argued with her about how good it was. How she wished to have him there and have such a silly argument again. She began reading.

Dearest Mary,

If you're reading this, I'm already building our home in heaven. Don't worry, it will be exactly as your journal says you want it to be. I wish we had more time together. Every moment we had together was filled with a lifetime of joy. I had not had much fear in my life until our first sanctioned date. My only fear from that day on is whether I'd lose you. I hate myself for putting you through this because I can only imagine how excruciating it is, but I hope you understand why I had to do what I had to do. I lived a thousand lifetimes in my imagination with you and our family. And every single one of them was perfect, not because the life we lived was perfect but because you were in it, and a life lived with you can be nothing short of perfect. There are things about you others don't get to see. Your little idiosyncrasies that I absolutely fell in love with. Sure, you were the most beautiful girl in every room you were in with your gorgeous hair and your eyes

AIDAN HINTZE

I could swim in for all eternity. But it was the imperfections, the way your lip would quiver when you would make a joke and be unsure if people would laugh, the way you would sometimes forget what you were talking about and just start laughing, the way you would smile at me from across a room, or the way you would fall asleep in my arms. Or (don't tell the guys about this) the times I would fall asleep with my head in your lap and you talking to me. My favorite thing about you, though, was your faith in us. I have always had faith in God but never another person, until you. Your faith in us as a couple and in me as a man gave me strong faith in you. I may be gone now, but I'm only gone physically. I will be watching over you. And if God answered my prayer last night, the same prayer I have prayed every night since we moved to that first house outside of the city, then you might be pregnant. If you are, know you won't be alone. When it gets tough, pray, and I will be there. I will always be there for you both. Mary, you were my joy in a world that had fallen apart. I used to wish the world had never fallen apart. And then I met you, and if the world had to fall apart for me to meet you, then so be it. I will always love you.

PS I know how you said your happiest memories from childhood were Christmases covered in snow, so I wrote you this.

Good times will come and go,
our lives are subject to the winds as they blow,
with you every day was a Christmas covered in snow
I will love you forever, I hope you know.

CHAPTER 45

R U I Z

Ruiz began to wake up, realizing he was chained to a wooden post. He took account of his surroundings. He saw most of his security detail dead, but two of them alive were chained to the same post he was on. He asked them what happened. They told him that when the battle began to turn, they tried to rush him out of there, but a grenade went off nearby, and it knocked Ruiz unconscious. They tried dragging him, but it was no use, so the only way to protect him was to surrender.

Ruiz was beside himself. One of the most powerful men in the world was captured by a group of traitors who hid in the mountains. A man walked up and introduced himself to Ruiz as Michael. He had the prisoner detail handcuff Ruiz and have him follow Michael. Ruiz was led into the division's main bunker where the headquarters was housed.

Ruiz was curious why he was allowed to see the apparatus, but he began to accept the fact that he likely wouldn't be leaving there alive. They boarded the train after traversing hundreds of feet underground. Ruiz was just as amazed as Mary was seeing the atmospheric conditions and the giant trees this far underground. He had always been a military man, but he also had a curious mind, and this ecosystem underground intrigued him.

They arrived at the headquarters, "This is the headquarters, if you'd even call it that?" thought Ruiz. "How are we losing to a group that plans everything in a room as miserable looking as this?" Michael told the detail to uncuff Ruiz and invited Ruiz to sit down. Ruiz did not know Michael, but he had heard of the division's leader, Samson. Ruiz asked Michael if Samson was away on a mission or why was it he was not greeting Ruiz.

Michael, visibly emotional at the question, told Ruiz that Samson fell at the liberation of Lexington. Ruiz stated that it was a shame; he knew Samson well and would have relished catching up with him. Ruiz could surmise by Michael's distorted facial reaction to that statement that he might not know everything about his beloved leader.

Michael began asking Ruiz about his troop placements and movements. Ruiz refused to answer, stating he would never betray his men. Michael assumed that would be the case, so he now instead began asking Ruiz about his upbringing and early life. Ruiz was born in Argentina, and his family owned a farm. He had an uncle who was a pilot, who would come by every once in a while and teach him about the cosmos. Under normal circumstances Ruiz didn't talk about his family but, knowing he was likely about to die, saw no reason not to reminisce.

Michael asked how his family was affected by the virus. Ruiz stated they weren't at all. Ruiz had already been a military man, and he was already tapped by the NWO to be a commander in their new military. This was a bit of a shock to Michael. The NWO didn't form until years after the virus, or so he believed. Ruiz again saw that same distorted face on Michael and this time began to prod.

Ruiz said, "You didn't know how planned out this new world was, did you?"

Michael answered, "No, they tapped you before the virus, but still, how did your family remain unaffected?"

"Everyone that they tapped they gave the antidote to, enough for our families too. Most joined just because we knew we could save our families."

"Why not tell everyone? You were already in the military. Surely, if you sounded the alarm, this could have stopped before it started," Michael said.

"Did you ask Samson that question?"

"What do you mean?"

Ruiz said, "I was far from the only one tapped early. Samson was one of the first to be chosen by the NWO. By the time they came to me, they had already had their European and North American contingents ready to go. My defiance would have just meant my family died along with the billions of others. Samson, however, he was one of the first one hundred tapped. So again, I ask, why didn't you ask him that question?"

Michael said, "I know this is a trick. You saw my emotional reaction about his death, so you're trying to paint him in a bad light and damage the ideal of this company in my mind."

"I'm merely speaking the truth. If that's damaging to your ideals, then that is between you and your God. I heard Colonel Anderson is assisting you all. Ask him. He, too, knew Samson very well."

"So if you knew Samson so well, did you two ever serve together?"

Ruiz replied, "Yes, we fought together in the Africa campaign, the German uprising, the first Texas uprising, and the Columbian uprising. He had quite the reputation."

"For what?"

"For slaughtering anyone who even looked at him the wrong way. Civilian, enemy combatant, even friendly soldiers. He killed thousands, this leader you have such emotional attachment to."

"That is most definitely a lie."

"I saw it with my own eyes, women, children. He would build a pyre in the middle of town squares. He would then find anyone with any affiliation to Christianity—tattoos, necklaces, what have you. He would let the men live as an example to other men, but he would take the man's wife and children, tie them to the pyre, and burn them alive. He said to me after one of the burnings with a chuckle, 'Some God they serve can't even stop one man from killing his women and children.'"

Michael said, "You must be confused. Samson was a devout Christian. He carried the Bible everywhere. He had the image of the cross tattooed on his chest and the upside-down cross in honor of Peter on his neck."

"No, Michael, it is you who seems to be confused. I have no doubt he changed. He turned on us, so he must have changed in some ways.

But you go ask your Colonel Anderson. He was with me in Columbia when Samson was burning them alive. Even I, who I'm sure you have your thoughts of, did not like the sights of what Samson did to the common people."

"All right, enough of that. If you won't give me useful information, I'm going to send you to your quarters."

"If you're going to kill me, just get on with it. I'm never going to give you the information you want, so let's not waste each other's time."

"I don't kill prisoners. I'm not like you, or how you perceive Samson to have been."

"It's not my perception. It's the reality. But all right, so take me to my cell."

"I will be seeing you soon."

Ruiz was escorted up to the ground flood and outside the bunker and to his quarters. To his surprise his quarters were a wooden home. He saw the same or similar-looking wooden homes everywhere and wondered if they were all prisoners too. He was greeted at the door by a counselor, who told him it was his new home now and began to explain the way of life among the division. Ruiz was confused. He was a prisoner of war, not a new member. But he said nothing because he was intrigued.

The counselor explained how the underground system, the ecosystem, and their barter system worked. Ruiz saw there was still a detachment of five Charlemagne men with him, so he knew this wasn't a mistake. It was a curious situation though for Ruiz. The house and the yard with the beautiful green grass were like something he had not seen in decades. He hadn't been outside an NWO big city metropolis since the outbreak began. It reminded him of his childhood on the farm.

The counselor asked if he wished to see the park, as it was close by. He wondered if he would be able to escape, but it seemed unlikely. Everywhere he went, the five men shadowed him, and there were guards posted almost every thirty feet, it seemed. The park was beautiful, and so many people were around one another, laughing, some singing and dancing even. He was dumbfounded. Ruiz never thought he would see something like this again in his lifetime, or anyone's for that matter. He was beginning to almost respect the division, for what they had been able to create.

The counselor asked if he had any questions, but Ruiz had already had most of them answered. Now he wished to just drink in the experience. He asked if he could go inside the park and sit on the bench alone. The counselor said he would leave him alone, but he couldn't promise the guards would. The guards, as Ruiz expected, continued to follow him. Ruiz was sitting in the sunlight on the park bench, drinking it in.

Ruiz then heard a loud scream and saw a man running at him aggressively. Ruiz did not have a weapon on him but was confident in his fighting abilities if the guards wanted to let this go. His confidence grew by the fact that this man running toward him was clearly malnourished and appeared to be 5'8" and maybe 120 lbs. The man got within twenty feet of Ruiz when two of the five guards grabbed him, and the other three cuffed Ruiz to the bench while they dealt with the scenario.

Ruiz wondered why the guards didn't let the man attack him knowing Ruiz's men killed many of the division's men. Knowing that Ruiz's men take no prisoners, they killed anyone surrendering. But he chalked it up to them being soft and this being a chief reason why they would lose the war.

Ruiz was uncuffed and escorted home. They barred the doors to lock him inside. He shrugged and decided to go to sleep, wondering if he would wake up again.

CHAPTER 46

MICHAEL

Michael was astonished and in awe of the civilians who defied the alarm bells and fought. He was looking around to make sure his men were all good when he saw Andrae. Andrae should not be there; he was an intelligence asset, not a regular soldier. He went over to Andrae to ask him why he was there, and Andrae told him they all came to follow Jeff. Michael asked where Jeff was, and Andrae said he didn't know, as they got separated during the battle, and he couldn't find him.

Michael told his men to look for Jeff; it was their priority. Within minutes one of his men was screaming that he found Jeff. Michael and Andrae ran over. Jeff had three bullet wounds to his stomach, two to his chest, and four in his legs. He was lying in a puddle of his own blood, which was growing rapidly. Michael screamed for a medic, but Jeff told him there was no point and not to waste the supplies on him. He was not going to make it.

Jeff told Michael to tell Mary that he was sorry and that now he could protect her always from above. Andrae had tears in his eyes, wiping them away, but Michael sat there holding on to Jeff, praying with him and telling him they would meet again soon. Jeff faded away within seconds, almost as if he was holding on just to get that final message to Mary.

Michael found out Mary was in the hospital, so he and Andrae headed that way. Upon arriving, Michael saw all of Jeff and Mary's friends. He didn't know them all personally, so he introduced himself and waited with the rest of them until the nurse said they could go in and see Mary.

Michael told Mary what Jeff said, tried to be as comforting as possible, and let his tears show when consoling her. Michael never knew what leadership was truly like. He saw Samson leading but never truly grasped the burden. They had won a great victory against the South America NWO today, but he felt nothing but grief. Not just for Jeff but for everyone who died under his command and for all the civilians. Samson would often quip "Heavy lies the crown." Now Michael was truly starting to feel the weight of that crown of leadership.

While leaving the hospital, Michael was informed that they were able to capture Ruiz. More good news on a sad day. Michael went to the location where Ruiz was being held captive and spoke with him.

Michael had an unsavory conversation with Ruiz. He didn't believe the things Ruiz told him about Samson to be true; it must be a ruse of some sort. But what would Ruiz truly gain by saying those lies? It just didn't make sense. How could Samson have been that evil formerly and then become the great man he was as the leader. The man who turned on the NWO to save civilians, the man who never allowed prisoners to be mistreated, the man who prayed with everyone, the man who literally gave his own clothes to others to keep them warm, the man who consoled everyone and never once had a complaint. How could it be possible?

Michael planned to ask Colonel Anderson about it, but that would be a conversation for another day. He had a plan with Ruiz. He was going to show Ruiz the true way of life in the division. He knew Ruiz wouldn't rat on his men or those he was loyal to. Michael firmly believed their way of life could turn him. Similar to a movie he had watched in his youth, *The Last Samurai*, which was based on a true story, the story was of a French military trainer hired by a Japanese clan to help fight another. The Frenchman was taken prisoner by those he was paid to fight but fell in love with their way of life and ended up training and fighting alongside them against his former allegiances.

Michael's plan might not work, and Spear was against it. Spear thought they should publicly execute Ruiz, as a revenge for all those Ruiz killed, including civilians. While Michael did believe there needed to be a punishment for these acts, he also believed they could still gain insight from Ruiz.

Michael was back at his quarters when he heard a knock. He answered the door and saw two guards with a cuffed skinny male. He was informed by the guards that the man charged at Ruiz, and they wished to know what Michael wanted done with him. Michael told them to uncuff the man and invited the man to sit on his couch.

The man told Michael his name was David.

Michael said, "The David who just joined the military and is being referred to as the lamb for your actions at the battle?"

David answered, "Yes. Why is that man allowed to live? I saw him execute two civilians."

Michael asked, "You witnessed this yourself?"

Michael could see David was becoming emotional.

"Yes. They were my friends, my only friends. They were unarmed, and they were murdered. He shot them in the head and chuckled as he did it." David began to cry.

Michael said, "I'm sorry that happened, and I promise you we will avenge your friends and everyone, military member and civilian, who died. But he does have a lot of useful information, so for now we need him alive and unharmed."

David said, "And free to walk around the park they died trying to protect? That they will never be able to see again?"

Michael said, "I understand how difficult that is, and I will be the first to admit it is not just, but as I'm sure you well know, we do not live in a just world. The righteous and just thing to do would be to listen to my commander, Spear, and execute him. But the knowledge he has can save our people in the future engagements. It can make it so no more Jack's and Katie's die. So while it is not just, it is what must be for right now. Let me ask you, if the story I'm told is true, you only came here recently, after the liberation of Lexington. Correct?"

David said, "Yes."

"Why not come before? Many did, and you would have had the same opportunities as them."

"I believed what I was being told was the truth."

Michael said, "Okay, if you believed that, then surely, you have made some mistakes in your life, no?"

David said, "I never murdered any…Well, I never executed anyone."

Michael asked, "Why did you stop what you were saying? I'm not someone you need to fear. You can tell me what you meant."

David replied, "Well, when I was living in Lexington, there were the antipet laws, and I saw a boy with a pet, so I reported him. I did not know what would happen."

Michael asked, "What did happen?"

David answered, "I saw the mother the following day. She told me they killed her boy and sent her his ashes."

Michael asked, "And do you believe you are beyond redemption for that?"

David answered, "Yes, there is no redemption for me."

Michael said, "I disagree. I only know of you because the entire division has heard your story. The story of the lamb, they're all calling it. They called it that because of how thin and small you are, but if they knew this, this redemption story of yours, it would be even more meaningful. A great man asked me once, is it better to be born a good man or to be born an evil man but battle with and defeat that evil every day? Now I'm not saying you were born evil, but we can both agree I imagine you've done some things that led to and perpetrated evil. But then you also did what you did yesterday, fought for something bigger than yourself, saved lives and gave hundreds of thousands of people hope. So if you ask me, David, not only are you redeemable. God has already redeemed you."

David looked up at the mention of God.

He said, "I had never really thought about God, just would laugh and make fun of any who believed in him. But when I was there and I saw Jack and Katie get executed, something or someone was speaking to me. I was not acting alone. I wish I was, but I'm not brave enough for that."

Michael said, "None of us are. We all are helped by those around us and from him above us. Just because you have a troubled past doesn't mean he is not willing and able to walk alongside you and carry you when necessary. He spoke to you, so maybe now it's your turn to speak to him."

David asked, "How do you know it was God though?"

Michael answered, "Well, who else would it have been? It wasn't me."

David and Michael both laughed at that.

David asked, "Why would God help me? Why would he want anything to do with me? Jack was braver than me, so was Katie. Both believed in him. Both were bigger, stronger."

Michael said, "I can't say what his plans are or why he chooses who he does for the tasks he chooses them for. What I can say from reading the Bible and my own personal experiences, though, is that he seems to pick those we would all least expect, and maybe that is by design. Someone like you with your story can lead others to him. I don't think it's a coincidence that the men here have nicknamed you the lamb, and that is what God is often referred to as."

David asked, "You have a Bible? I thought they were all destroyed."

Michael answered, "Many were but not all, and we have made our own printing press and began remaking as many as we can, but yes, I have multiple. I will give you one."

David asked, "Where would I start?"

Michael said, "Do what I do—start from the beginning, but if you're having a particularly tough day, pray, ask for a sign, and then open it up randomly and read whatever page it is on."

David said, "Thank you. I will. How long will Ruiz be kept alive for?"

Michael replied, "Until he gives us the information we need."

David said, "And then you'll kill him, you swear?"

Michael said, "The only way I won't is if you plead for his life. That, I swear to you."

David said, "Well, then he will surely die. Thank you, sir, and sorry about today."

Michael said, "You are a hero of this division. You have nothing to apologize for. Before you leave, lamb, can I share your story with the men? Your true story?"

David asked, "You don't think they'll hate me for it?"

Michael said, "I think many of them have the same struggles, and they will love you for it."

David said, "Okay, I leave for training with my unit tomorrow. If I'm gone long, please wait till I get back to kill him. I'd love to be the one to tie the noose, but if not, I want to watch him die."

Michael said, "That is a deal. I will see you soon, lamb."

"No one is beyond redemption," Michael remembered Samson telling him that once when Michael asked him why they treated the captured NWO soldiers so well knowing what would happen to them if they got caught. Even from the grave, Samson was still teaching Michael how to lead. Maybe what Ruiz said was true, but why would Samson hide that from him? Michael wondered.

He then realized for the same reason David didn't want the men to know about his past, which paled in comparison. Samson knew how he was perceived, and he probably wanted to keep that perception. If everyone knew about his murderous past, they might be more akin to commit atrocities themselves, not knowing the burden it would leave on their soul. He still wasn't sure he believed it, but it was starting to feel like it was the truth.

CHAPTER 47

DAVID

David was still trying to make sense of everything. His entire worldview was flipped on its head, and then his two closest friends, only friends, were murdered in front of him. Something took over him, and he began killing those he once thought of as heroes. David was with the counselor, trying to explain it all in a sensible manner.

David said, "I don't understand what could have compelled me to do what I did."

Anthony said, "It was the love you have for your friends. Love is the most powerful of all emotions. It makes people do all sorts of things. Some terrible, some great, but what you did would definitely fall into the great category"

David said, "It doesn't feel great. I killed people."

"Anthony; There is a difference in killing people for conquest and killing people to protect others. While you may not have had the conscious thought of why you were killing those NWO soldiers, your actions saved lives. Further, it inspired those around you to fight harder, which also saved lives."

David said, "I still don't understand, though. It was as if I wasn't even doing it. Like someone else or something else had taken control of me."

Anthony said, "Well, that is something the local religious leaders could probably speak more to. I was never a particularly religious person myself, but after living here long enough and hearing enough of these stories, it's hard for me to deny God's presence, which I would bet is what that voice was that took over."

David asked, "Why is everyone saying that? Why would God speak to me and not Katie or Jack?"

Anthony said, "Again, those are questions I cannot answer. What I can say is you've lived in big cities all your life. So maybe this isn't the first time he spoke to you but rather the first time you could hear him."

David left the counselor's office feeling more confused than before he went in. But he couldn't dwell on that today was to be his first day of training, and he only had thirty minutes to get to the barracks.

David arrived at the barracks and was told he had been assigned to Lima platoon. Most of the platoon had already undergone their initial training phase, yet all of them were there, waiting to meet him. A tall but skinny man approached David, squintingly looked him up and down, and said, "I guess the nickname fits. I'm Rodger, your platoon leader."

Rodger took David aside and explained to him that even though he was seen as some hero, he wouldn't be given any special privileges and would have to pass the training requirements like everyone else, which would be hard for a boy of his size. David said he understood and wouldn't want to be treated differently. Rodger walked out of the barracks, and David was left with forty-three men and women staring at him.

A man named Walter walked up to him, introduced himself, and handed him two small black pieces of fabric, which were patches. David was unsure what they were, but there was writing on them. Before David could begin reading them, Walter started to explain the platoon had those made for everyone, and they were all excited to wear them when the training was finished, and they were sent to the line and to combat.

David read the first one, with a black background and a bright blue lettering, "Fear the Lamb." The second piece of fabric with the same color scheme read, "Rise and rise again until Lambs become Lions." Walter then explained that there were only five platoons in this company, but they requested to change theirs from Bravo to Lima, *L* for Lamb. Walter told David, "Most of the soldiers in this platoon were there at the gate the day you earned your nickname." David then looked around and saw every single soldier was wearing those patches on either shoulder.

David was overwhelmed; he had never known more than two people who had ever cared about him, and he felt like it was out of sympathy. Now he had battle-hardened soldiers who were waiting to meet him, who made him gifts, and who were looking at him like he was some hero. In reality he still felt like a coward, the same coward who got that woman's son killed, the same coward who chose to question nothing and believe everything he was told, the same coward who, after being shown the truth and his only friends in the world wanted to join the division and fight, he still wouldn't. He didn't understand how all these brave, strong people could see in him something so far from the truth. So he accepted the gifts, said thank you, and just got ready for training. It wasn't that he didn't want to thank everyone individually or he wanted to be rude; he simply felt unworthy of this, of all of it.

The training was supposed to take four weeks, but it had been three, and the six Lima platoon new recruits were all performing well above standards. This was likely because it was the only platoon that had all forty-three of its members in every single day of the basic training. Even though thirty-seven of them had already passed, they were there helping the others and going through it all again. The difference was very noticeable at the company level, particularly in the camaraderie between the Lima platoon and the others.

Because of this, on day one of the fourth week of training, Rodger addressed the platoon. They had been tasked with a special mission. They were to link up with Colonel Anderson's mechanized units and provid forward scouting and, if necessary, guerilla attacks on the South American contingents still in North America. The soldiers were exuberant at the news, even David, which confounded him even more. He had felt himself change so much in the past six months since the liberation. It was as if he was a totally unrecognizable person. Still, he felt that he was unworthy of the praise the other soldiers continued to throw his way. He had been reading the Bible Michael gave him every day, but that usually just made him feel even more sorrowful about his cowardly past. He prayed that during this campaign, he could do something great enough to make him respect the man in the mirror.

It took Lima platoon about one week to finally link up with Anderson's mechanized units. They were hugging the coastline of the Gulf of Mexico down by the Florida-Alabama border. Colonel Anderson's units had already scored multiple victories against the South American rear guard, but they were reinforced and set up a defensive line from Louisiana to California.

Upon linking up, Colonel Anderson noticed the patches everyone was wearing, looked at David, who was noticeably smaller than everyone else, and stated, "So you're this lamb we've all heard so much about?"

David said, "Yes. Happy to meet you, sir."

Colonel Anderson said, You as well. Me and my men left everything to fight for the oppressed. It's always welcome to see them joining the fight too."

David then left, and Rodger and Anderson talked. David went back to the makeshift barracks the platoon had set up and was hanging out with the others. He didn't feel like an outsider here, but he still felt like a phony, underserving of their love and admiration. He tried his best to hide it, but many saw through it.

Rodger came back and told them they would leave at nightfall, and they were to probe the enemy's defensive line to see if there was a weak spot. Rodger told the men to try to get some rest now because they would be up all night, and likely some of them wouldn't make it back. David wasn't expecting a speech like that, but with all that had happened, he didn't fear death anymore.

Nightfall arrived. The platoon was outfitted by Anderson's men with three Humvees, two fast-moving lightweight ATVs, and two Armored Personnel Carriers (APC) with a 40 mm turret on top. Each Humvee held five men, the two fast movers held four mean, and each APC held ten men. The fast-moving ATVs provided the least protection but did have one M240 machine gun and an automatic grenade launcher on either side of the back seats. The fast movers were also the quietest, so Rodger devised a plan in which they would essentially be sent out to do the recon and drive as close as possible to enemy positions before being found, and if they found a spot they think could easily be punched through, they would call for the APCs and Humvee's.

The plan wasn't well received, but it was followed. David requested to be in one of the ATVs, which gave a morale boost for all those around him. The plan was working in the sense that they were able to get very close to the line of defense without being noticed. They had identified three potential weak points along the Alabama border. They were continuing north to see if there were more when Rodger called them back. He liked one of the weak points they found, so he wanted them all to meet at the rendezvous point so he could devise a plan to break through that line and hold position for Anderson.

Rodger's plan now would have one APC and the Humvees spearheading the assault while the ATVs started pumping rounds at either side of the spearhead to make it seem like they were a much larger force. The second APC would maintain the initial line they took and repel any counterattacks. The men had a last meal, some prayed, David read his Bible, and then it was time to move.

Initial contact went as planned, the recon intel was correct, and there were only two machine gun nests that were not fortified and no antiarmor at this spot. Rodgers radioed to Anderson that he found a weak spot, and Anderson replied they were on their way with the battalion. The feign attacks to the north and south were also working; NWO soldiers could be seen retreating for miles to come. Lima platoon hunkered down in their position and began building fortifications and trenches in case a counterattack came before Anderson's mechanized units.

The tanks could be heard for miles as the heavies of Anderson's battalion began arriving. It was a beautiful sight to all of Lima but to David most of all because he saw something familiar written on the barrel of the lead tank: "For we do not wrestle against flesh and blood, but against principalities, against powers, against the rulers of the darkness of this age, against spiritual hosts of wickedness in the heavenly places." David was still new to the faith, and he didn't understand why seeing this was having such a profound effect on him, but it was.

Rodger gathered the men and told them Anderson's battalion was going to continue through and engage the South American contingent further west. Lima platoon's mission was to hold this gap in their line so Anderson's battalion could fall back if needed. David and the men look at one another with a sense of relief and pride. They have zero doubt that Anderson's battalion would make short work of the South American military.

The battle could be heard raging from a distance. The massive artillery barrages, and the tanks exploded. From this distance it was impossible to know who was winning, but the platoon had full faith they would be able to rest easy tonight.

At the break of dawn, the battle could still be heard raging, but now it sounded like it was getting closer. Then as if out of nowhere, the skies became filled with NWO aircraft. They began slicing through Anderson's mechanized units. Now Lima platoon was watching in horror as the best among them were in full retreat being cut down by enemy helicopters and bombers. The plan didn't involve much antiaircraft or fighter support from the coast because the weather reports indicated heavy storms. They didn't think the NWO would risk their aircraft in bad weather.

Anderson's men reached Lima platoon and rushed past them to get to their fortified lines, which were close enough to the coasts, to get fighter support. Rodgers asked Anderson what he wanted Lima platoon to do. Anderson said, "Hold the point until the tanks make it through. We need to save our tanks." Rodgers acknowledged the order and relayed it to the men and women of Lima.

The pride and joy were swept off their faces. What was an assured victory had turned into an assured defeat and possibly an assured death. Rodgers informed them that they would retreat with all haste once the last tank of Anderson got close, but until then they must cover their retreat. Some of Anderson's men chose to join Lima company on their own. Anderson was reluctant, but they were not going to take no for an answer. This gave the Lima soldiers some hope of survival.

The battle was raging on. The South American artillery and air bombardments were relentless, only stopping for thirty-minute intervals where another contingent of combined mechanized/infantry arms would try to push their position. The original forty-three was already cut down to twenty, and of the fifty of Anderson's men who chose to hold the point, only thirty remained.

Rodgers was unsure of what to do, but he didn't want his entire platoon slaughtered, so he ordered a retreat. Anderson's men, assuming the order was coming from Anderson, did not object, but David did. Rodgers was perplexed and a bit enraged by this, stating he must listen to his superior, to which David responded no. David stated he would remain and hold this point as long as he could so they could all make it to safety.

This act had all the remaining men from Anderson and all the remaining soldiers from Lima defying Rodgers's order. They all wished to stay with the lamb. Rodgers saw no point in dying for no reason, so he retreated by himself. The fighting intensified.

David pleaded with the others to fall back, stating it was hopeless to continue, and he wished to save their lives by remaining. After the last tank passed through safely, Anderson's men said they should all fall back now, which David again refused. He said if they all left at once, none would survive, so he asked to be left alone to hold the ground. Six of Lima platoon and three of Anderson's men decided to stay with David. Ten would be enough to hold them back and save the rest.

Samuel, one of Anderson's men, asked David why he was so willing to die there.

David said, "To redeem the sins of my past and to hopefully be able to think of myself as a coward no longer."

Samuel said, "I don't know what you have done in your past, but surely, you are not a coward, and any man willing to do what you are about to will not only have heaven's gates opened at your arrival but will have a host of your ancestors waiting to greet you."

Tears began to well in David's eyes.

David, said, "'Greater love hath no man than this, that a man lay down his life for his friends.' I read that passage right before the battle.

I now see how everything happens for a reason. Thank you for your words, Samuel."

Samuel said, "No, thank you, sir. And I will see you again soon. Make ten soldiers feel like a thousand."

Samuel, the rest of Anderson's men, and the rest of Lima platoon retreated in the vehicles. They heard from behind them a glorious ruckus of gunfire. They knew their fellow soldiers wouldn't make it, but they would not be forgotten.

CHAPTER 48

BOLTON

Bolton's aides found him as giddy as could be after broadcasting Winters's death to Dietrich and the upper echelons of the rebels. Bolton felt as though he had won the war with this move, especially now that the other continents' men had arrived. They would have ten times the manpower that was defending the West.

Bolton ordered the Felix legions to use any means necessary to form a breakthrough at a point in the northern end of the western wall. While this was close to what remained of the rebel navy in that area, Bolton felt they would least expect the attack there.

Bolton had his main regular forces sent to the southern part of the wall. He intended to try to do a massive pincer movement, entrapping those defending the wall in between the two points of entry. At which point he would let them starve, cut off from supplies, and if any resistance was given, the bomber squadrons would get a turkey shoot.

For once Bolton's generals agreed with his plans and dispatched the orders to their men. Bolton then pulled aside Lieutenant Commander Jocko, leader of the Felix legions, and told him killing Dietrich was a priority but to try to keep his body intact. He wished to display it like he did Winters's. Jocko was an interesting man to pick for this mission, considering before the Felix Legions were formed, he served directly under Dietrich. Jocko agreed to the order but wondered if he wasn't being tested himself.

The march west was slow, bogged down by rain and equipment delays. Even the advancements in technology that had been made over the years couldn't seem to stop the timeless fogs of war.

Bolton was bringing with him any and all civilians who are suspected of helping the western advance east. He knew the western NWO would have brought them all with them west of the lines, but some of the family members might have wished to stay loyal to the NWO. They should have taught their family members better than to be traitors. He felt no remorse for what was about to happen to them.

Finally, they reached the western fortifications. To his surprise they had not been slowed down by aircraft. While on the southern end, the NWO would have a clear advantage; to the north, with the rebel navy in the English Canal, they could have done serious damage to the Felix legions. It was something Bolton was counting on. He wanted to bleed the legions dry because after this war, there would be no more need for them.

Bolton's excitement was palpable as they arrived at their forward command post. His top generals knew why, but not everyone in the room did. He gave a final decree: no one in the West was to be left alive. Now the last battle for Europe began.

CHAPTER 49

DIETRICH

Dietrich learned of the advance West. He ordered his navy taken from the channel and sent to the coasts of Normandy and France to take every civilian to the American rebel strongholds. He also sent all the aircraft he had left. He had four of his own personal guard go to bring his wife to safety. He knew she wouldn't leave willingly, so he told them they could tranquilize her. He would die at his post if he must, but she would live on.

Dietrich knew Bolton well, and he knew he would throw everything he had at the western wall. So Dietrich left but a splinter force defending England, sent the entire fleet across the Atlantic as well as the bulk of his ground forces, but handpicked his top mechanized and infantry divisions to defend the western wall.

Dietrich also knew Bolton would do something to try to appeal to the humanity of the western soldiers. So a decree was issued, saying that anyone seen to the east would be shot, whether civilian or NWO. His generals and the men did not like this; they were fighting as liberators, not people who murdered civilians. Nonetheless, the order was given.

By the scouts' estimations, and thanks to heavy rains, they had approximately three days to fortify their positions and prepare. Dietrich had assembled a myriad of defensive positions and traps. He knew with the numbers they were facing, defeat was almost a foregone conclusion, but they could enact a godly number of casualties on their foe, thus making a trip across the Atlantic near impossible.

The day of the battle had arrived. To the surprise of the men and Dietrich himself, they were not getting relentlessly bombed or struck with heavy artillery. They saw movement on the front, but it wasn't soldiers. It was civilians running toward the line with their hands in the air, screaming for help. Dietrich repeated his order for everyone to be shot. He knew it was a trap, but this order fell on deaf ears.

Dietrich raised his own rifle, got a sight picture, but couldn't take the shot. He knew this was part of a plan, and it was working, but he intended to die with his soul intact. If that was even possible anymore, he thought. Dietrich ordered his men to stand down but be ready and shoot at the first white helmet they saw.

Some of the civilians were making it through to the line of fortifications. They were immediately transported to the first aid stations behind the front. It was midday, and still no military, just a constant stream of civilians.

Then a massive explosion was heard behind the line, and another, and another. Almost as if on cue, now the skies opened up with heavy artillery.

While he couldn't be sure, Dietrich thought he knew what it meant. He knew Bolton was a cold SOB, but he figured one of the civilians would have warned them. The only logical explanation was they put bombs inside the civilians knowing they'd be taken to the first aid station. Now Dietrich's wounded would have nowhere to go. "No matter," Dietrich thought, "he just burned our boats."

When the artillery barrage ended, the first waves of NWO tanks and infantry appeared. They expected to face a softened foe, but they were mistaken. The Western European (W.E) continental forces were always seen as the highest quality in the military, and the other continental forces were learning the reason for that now.

Every shot by a W.E soldier was expertly placed, hitting its target. The eastern tanks were being shredded by the western antitank guns. The W.E hadn't even begun to use their own tanks. It did not take long for the NWO continental forces to break off and flee. Then they skies turned black.

Bombers as far as the eye could see, Dietrich had all his men put on their chemical suits. He couldn't be certain, but he wouldn't put it past

Bolton to use nuclear warheads even this early on. The bombing was relentless, but the fortifications held strong.

There were some casualties taken, but the WE won the day and had inflicted massive casualties on the NWO troops. Dietrich received hopeful news: Jocko and the spearhead of the Felix legion had turned on the others. Jocko's legion was now fighting the remaining two Felix legions outside the walls on the northern end.

Dietrich made a risky but desperate call and ordered his mechanized units in the north to engage and support Jocko's men. This was a suicide mission from the beginning. But if they could turn some of the eastern armies against themselves, maybe there was a chance.

The combined force of the W.E mechanized units and Jocko's Felix legion was able to easily overtake the other two Felix Legions. Dietrich ordered them to fall back and be added to the defensive line, but the Felix Legions, and Jocko in particular, were not fond of following orders they disagreed with. The mechanized units began to fall back, but the legion now pressed southbound, engaging NWO continental men and making easy work of them considering they hadn't established strong defenses on their flanks.

Dietrich saw this and ordered his central and northern tank commands to push forward with the legion. This could work. As the night raged on, the sounds and muzzle flashes were deafening and blinding to the men still holding the line at the wall. They could only imagine the horrors those in the center of it all were facing. They couldn't tell who was winning, but they had faith in the quality of their men over the NWO men, no matter the odds.

CHAPTER 50

BOLTON

Bolton was enraged by the betrayal. He wanted the Felix legions destroyed anyway but not at the cost of his northern front. His aides pleaded for rational thinking and a counteroffensive with some of the central armies. But Bolton did not deal well with betrayal.

The manpower advantage the NWO contingents had was astounding; a counteroffensive would surely overtake the western mechanized units and the disloyal Felix Legion. But Bolton wanted to send a message, not just to the West but also to his own men.

Bolton ordered all the heavy artillery and bombers to shell everything north of the central army. His generals and aides were beside themselves. There were still hundreds of thousands of NWO soldiers up there fighting. They would all be killed by their own side. Bolton did not care; if his men were going to die, they would die at his hand, not Dietrich's or Jocko's. The faces on the high command were unforgettable, but the orders were followed.

Everything north was turned into a massive ball of flame. Unbeknownst to his generals and aides, Bolton ordered the air command to use napalm. He knew the fighting was close to the wall, and he wanted those defending it to hear the screams of the fate they would soon face.

Now with the screams still fresh in the defenders' mind, Bolton ordered a massive push on the south end of the wall. Bolton was in the command post when he learned of the intricate defenses the wall possessed. He expected it to be formidable, but with only three days' time to lay traps and mines, he wasn't expecting it to cause as many casualties as it was.

Bolton continued to throw all his manpower against the wall while also ordering napalm strikes behind the wall. He had nuclear warheads and would use them if necessary, but the wall was situated on one of the few fertile landscapes left in the world and was necessary to feed the world population. The NWO parliamentary body had stated that nukes were not allowed to be used here.

Bolton listened for now, but he also knew those under his command would do whatever he told them. So while the parliament might think they had the power, truly, Bolton would have the final decision.

Wave after wave crashed against the wall and were thrown back. Every man caught retreating was shot on sight by the rear guards of the NWO.

Day four of this battle, Bolton was becoming increasingly agitated. With their superior armaments and manpower, they should have been through the wall already. Bolton's generals knew what was on his mind, but they hoped he didn't do it.

Bolton called his head of security to his office at the forward command post. Bolton's head of security was the lieutenant commander in charge of all NWO security forces. Bolton ordered him to execute Operation Benedict. He left the room along with two communications personnel.

Bolton's command staff reentered with seemingly frightened looks. Everyone believed they were the good guy in their own story, but if Bolton was about to order what they thought he was, it would be hard to convince themselves of that when they tried to sleep tonight.

Bolton confirmed the generals' fears; he was going to nuke the wall and all the West. But that was not all. As they were speaking, the parliament of the NWO was being executed by the security forces under Bolton's command. He told his generals that while this task of nuking the West was certainly distasteful, it would lead to a better world—a world where they no longer had to take orders from a supposed elected official, a world where might equaled power, and every general in that room would have their power immensely bolstered and insulated. The mood changed; now the generals saw the immense benefits not only for themselves and their families but also for what they perceived would be benefits they could impart on the world.

Bolton had succeeded, as always, at getting his men to do whatever bidding he wished.

CHAPTER 51

DIETRICH

Dietrich joined with his commanders and men in hoping, believing that their tanks with the Felix Legion could turn the tide and win the day. The fighting was intense, but the reports coming in to the CP, which Dietrich had on the wall itself, were all bearing good news: victory after victory with minimal casualties.

The battle raged on; constant counterattacks by the NWO were thrown back by the superior tactics and training of the western units. Then a bright flash was seen where the battle was being hardest fought. Dietrich knew Bolton was using nukes. He had only minutes, seconds maybe, to send out a message to Anderson and those on the American front: "America is the last hope. Fortify the defenses, and defend everyone you can. We have been good men. We have been bad men. As Winston Churchill famously said, 'Not every great man is a good man.' Now it is time for us to become great men. Colonel, I will see you again."

The contingency was set into motion: all naval air assets were directed to strike South American targets to buy the rebels time. Dietrich died on the western front but not before sending a last message to his wife, thanking her for the beautiful life they lived together and asking for forgiveness for leaving her now.

CHAPTER 52

THE LIGHT AT THE END OF THE TUNNEL

Even though the location of their encampment was surely compromised, the decision was made to stay. They could try to find a suitable place to the north and replicate this civilization they had built, but it would take close to a decade. Also, the harsh Canadian winter, while being chased by NWO contingents, did not seem like a good idea to the leadership. With the massive aerial bombardment on the remaining South American positions as Dietrich's last order, they knew they had bought themselves time before another attack would be made against their mountain encampment. So defenses were being erected that would make the Maginot Line pale in comparison. Unlike the Maginot Line, they were not leaving any gaps.

The naval forces under the command of the rebels were more powerful than all the other contingents combined, so they were protected from a naval landing. The only way for the NWO to strike would be by land from South America. Knowing this, any rebel group willing was asked to set up a defensive line at the tightest point of Central America. The rebels wouldn't have the numbers, but they did have the more advanced tanks and ships. Also, with all the civilians who were able to escape Western Europe, they had now built a massive industrial capability. It could not match number for number the NWO contingents, but it was enough to hold grounds and launch counteroffensives to hold North America. The rebels had realized they didn't need to launch attacks and strike out on NWO territories. They knew the laws in those lands. One child per family, and most didn't even do that. In two generations' time, North

America would be more populous than the rest of the world. Time was now on the rebels' side, as long as they could defend America.

ABOUT THE AUTHOR

Aidan Hintze, author of *2035*, hails from a small town and a large family. His diverse professional background spans Law Enforcement, Airspace, Service industry, Retail, Marketing, and Construction. Aidan's passion for writing was born from his love for reading and a divine inspiration. His unique life experiences and interactions with people from various walks of life have enriched his creative writing. Aidan's work will resonate with critical thinkers, religious individuals, and fans of Orwell's *1984*. His writing challenges conventional narratives and invites readers to question established truths, reflecting his own questioning spirit and profound understanding of human nature.

Milton Keynes UK
Ingram Content Group UK Ltd.
UKHW012313040624
443649UK00007B/591